Make Me

CHARLOTTE STEIN

T0337268

mischief

Mischief
An imprint of HarperCollins*Publishers*
77–85 Fulham Palace Road,
Hammersmith, London W6 8JB

www.mischiefbooks.com

A Paperback Original 2013

First published in Great Britain in ebook format by
HarperCollins*Publishers* 2012

Copyright © Charlotte Stein 2012

Charlotte Stein asserts the moral right to
be identified as the author of this work

A catalogue record for this book is
available from the British Library

ISBN-13: 9780007534722

Set in Sabon by FMG using Atomic ePublisher from Easypress

Find out more about HarperCollins and the environment at
www.harpercollins.co.uk/green

CONTENTS

Contents

Chapter One

I think I'm a little stoned, so it's not a surprise that I hardly react when Brandon kisses the nape of my neck, all hot and wet. But it *is* a surprise that I don't react when he suddenly lifts my top up and exposes my bare breasts to Tyler's waiting gaze.

Yeah, that's a surprise, all right. Mainly because it's Brandon being so shockingly forceful, but also due to the fact that I can't quite recall why I didn't wear a bra tonight.

So they would see you, my mind throws up, but my mind is ridiculous. I don't want my best friends to see me, and they certainly don't want to look. They totally don't.

Except for all the parts where they totally do, because

when I glance up Tyler is running a gaze that seems suddenly heavy all over my naked tits, and Brandon has cupped one of said tits with a single too-large hand.

And I think – though cannot be sure – that he's making little noises. Little hot moans into the nape of my neck, followed by some breathy pants – of the kind that would usually arouse me. I mean, if this wasn't *Brandon* doing this I'd definitely be wet by now. Mainly because the sounds he's making are so hot and desperate and horny, but also because he doesn't take long to find one of my completely *not* stiff nipples and kind of … tug it a little.

As though he's just testing this whole thing out. Seeing if I'll mind, or something. And I guess I don't, because when he does it I make a sound of my own – though I swear I don't mean to. And I don't mean to shiver, either, when Tyler comes out with the following:

'Yeah, you like that, huh?'

In a voice that no longer sounds like his own. This new voice is really rough, like someone dragged a piece of sandpaper over it – though I'm not sure I'd understand what he's saying any better if he said it in his normal tone. He is talking about sex things, after all, and though he's likely just as semi-stoned as me – and God only knows how far gone Brandon is – there's something so wicked about that. So disturbing.

He expects me to answer him, and with words I've never used in front of either of them. And though I know what those words are – things like *mmmm* and *yeah* and *feels so good* – I can't quite do it.

Instead, I have to just lie there quietly in Brandon's arms, as he teases and toys with one nipple, and then the other. Fingers feverish and almost fumbling, sometimes falling into a kind of greedy squeeze of my heavy tits – like he thinks this whole thing is going to go away, soon. As if I'm just tolerating him fondling me, letting him get it out of his system before I put a stop to the whole thing.

But I'll be honest, I don't think the latter's going to happen. There's no urge in me to stop anything, despite the strange, almost uncomfortable silence we all seem to have fallen into. It's punctuated only by our combined heavy breathing, and I'm not sure how much longer I can take it without bursting out with something.

Or at least, I'm not sure until Tyler leans forwards and licks wherever Brandon isn't touching. After which, all the words I want to say – *we should really talk about this before we all start fucking* being chief amongst them – fall away inside me. Electric sparks of pleasure zip from my now unbelievably stiff nipples all the way down to places I don't want to discuss in polite company, and I make a sound instead of the sensible things I need to say.

A rough, dirty, moaning sort of sound. That gets louder when Brandon mutters, 'Yeah, suck it. Suck her nipple.'

I mean, Jesus. Where did he get *that* from? He's the sort of guy who can barely request that someone pass him the peas. He once pissed himself in primary school rather than ask the teacher if he could go to the bathroom. He shouldn't be telling his best friend to do that to me.

And his best friend shouldn't be obeying.

Because, oh, he does. He takes one tight peak in his mouth and sucks on it sloppily, messily, until I'm writhing and mindless and pulsing hard between my legs. My entire body has suddenly disappeared right down into my solid, aching clit, and worse than that, I think the pair of them know it.

They're both going at me so hard and greedy, and the moment I make any sort of move – a hand on the back of Tyler's head – he starts shoving my skirt up.

Of course, I immediately go bright red. Not because I don't want him to do it – because it would be ridiculous of me to deny it now – but because he's going to see, in a second. My dependable, no-nonsense friend Tyler is going to see that I've wet my panties, because he and my other friend are licking and sucking and rubbing my nipples.

I want to die of shame, I really do. And yet somehow, once he's got my skirt up and he's looking at me there, it's not half as bad as I had imagined. I know how rude it must look – the panties are just little cotton things, flimsy as anything, and I've made them so wet I can feel the material clinging to my swollen bud – but he does nothing to make me feel weird about it.

Quite the contrary. He groans and then, after a second of arranging me this way and that, rough hands on my thighs spreading me wider and wider, he says, 'Fuck, your clit's so big.'

And I swear, I feel nothing. Apart from intense arousal, of course.

It's so intense that I don't even protest when he gets hold of the material that's covering my slippery slit, and pulls it aside so he can get a better look. I just watch him, near breathless with anticipation, body now ready for anything while my mind takes a vacation.

'You want me to lick it?' he asks, and I don't know. It's like he's a different person, suddenly. Or maybe it's just that *I'm* a different person, because I find myself rolling my hips up at the fingers that refuse to do anything but hold that piece of elastic, while my mouth moves around words like: 'Ohhh yeah, yeah, lick my clit.'

Behind me, Brandon tenses – though I'm not sure why. Because I said a dirty thing? Because Tyler gets to go down on me, and he doesn't? I've no idea and quite frankly I can't care right at this moment, because Tyler's using those fingers for some purpose.

He pushes the elastic aside and then spreads my slit open, to expose my stiff clit – which doesn't sound very exciting, I know, but God, it *feels* exciting. It feels like the lewdest thing ever, coming from him, and it gets worse when he lets his thumb feather over the underside of my bud.

I arch my back. I can't help it. I'm right on the edge of some incredible orgasm, before he's even done anything at all. Just that little touch feels like something molten against my clit, and it spreads that heat all the way up and through my body.

'Man, look how ready she is,' he says, but Brandon doesn't say anything in reply. I think he's beyond words, to be honest, but that's OK. I am too. I want it so bad that I'm trying to put a sentence together – something like *Just rub me there, right now, just rub it, I'm gonna go off* – but it won't come.

Good job Tyler can speak for me, huh?

'You close, Maisie? Yeah, you're so close. Feel sweet when I do that?'

That being another agonising thumb-stroke over my clit.

'Uhhhhhh,' I say.

'How about this?' he asks, and then … oh God … then he slides a finger down through my slit to my ready and waiting hole.

It's like silk, going in. Almost as good as a cock, because, like everything on Tyler, his fingers are massive. So thick and long and good, and even better when he adds a second one and pumps, slowly.

'You want to know what she feels like?' he asks, and for a moment I have no idea what he's talking about. And then my brain catches up, and I realise he's asking Brandon. That this is a thing, this talking around me, and though Brandon can't say a word Tyler still knows he wants to hear all of this stuff.

'Ohhh, so wet and hot. So tight, too – she can barely take my two fingers. Can you imagine how small she'd feel around your cock?'

Again, my brain takes a moment to catch up. And when it does, it's not sure it wants to understand what Tyler is saying. My brain is apparently a prude, and hardly knows what to make of the fact that a) Tyler is aware that Brandon has a big cock, somehow and b) he doesn't think my tiny pussy could take it.

However, my body more than makes up for my prudish brain. My body is rocking on Tyler's fingers, and burying itself in Brandon's body, and there are all of these sounds coming out of my mouth.

'Just lick her,' Brandon says, hoarsely, and the sounds get louder. I have to push my face against the turn of his throat just to get them under control, though it's something of a lost cause once Tyler leans down to do as his friend is suggesting.

The first long, wet lick over my aching clit almost makes me clamp my legs back together. The pleasure is thick and jolting, almost like an orgasm but not quite.

Tyler backs off immediately, as though he knows how close I am and wants to drag this all out just a little longer. Just a little more of me squirming and embarrassing myself every time he gives me a little flick of his tongue and a little twist of his fingers inside me.

'Fuuuucccckk,' Brandon groans, and I have to say I know exactly how he feels. By the time Tyler starts lashing his tongue back and forth over the tip of my clit – barely touching, oh, such a tease – I'm delirious.

So much so that I fail to comprehend why Brandon is in such a state, too.

Only when I feel him against my side, all slick and firm and insistent, do I get it. I can make out the intermittent press of his hand, as he shuttles it up and down his obviously bare and very hard cock, and then, after a second of hardly daring to, I glance down and see what Tyler was talking about.

He's so big, so thick and solid and, fuck, it's hot. I've never been a size queen, but then again I've never seen anything like Brandon's cock, up close. I'm helpless in the face of it, and especially so when it's all swollen at the tip and glossy with pre-come and, oh Lord, I can't help urging him on. I can't, I can't.

'Yeah,' I tell him, and then other words stumble after it. 'Fuck yourself. Come on me, that's it. Come on me.'

I didn't even know that's what I wanted until the

words burst out. But now that they're out in the open, and we're all busy buried in each other's groins, I hardly think it matters. Brandon is going to spurt all over my belly and Tyler's going to get me off with his mouth and his hands and then afterwards he's probably going to come on me, too.

Or maybe I can be as daring as they seem to have been and take him in my mouth.

Would he like that? I can't tell. But I can definitely tell how much I like the thought of doing it – of sucking him until he fills my mouth with come – because I'm getting really close. He's stopped teasing and started lapping at me in earnest, fingers curling inside me so that they rub right up against that sensitive spot, and I can see my belly tightening. Can feel my thighs tensing and releasing, as pleasure builds at the base of my clit.

Though it isn't Tyler's expert sucking and fucking that pushes me over, I have to say. I mean, it feels good. And when he does this little curling thing with his tongue I nearly lose my mind. But even so, it's still Brandon whispering in my ear that gets me there.

'Are you gonna do it?' he asks, then closely after it: 'Tell me. I want to come when you do.'

I can feel him shuddering against me, hand working hard and mean on his slick cock, and something about that combination – his desire to hold off and his obvious intense need to come – makes my body sing. Makes me tell him: 'Oh fuck yeah, now, I'm coming, I'm coming – do it.'

And then he does, just as my clit swells against Tyler's tongue and pleasure unwinds inside me like a coil of electricity.

I don't know whom I cling to. I only know that I go completely rigid and grunt like an animal, as my orgasm pulses on and on and Brandon spurts thickly against my side. He moans gutturally as he does, but it has absolutely nothing on the sounds I make.

Or the sounds Tyler makes when he kneels up and starts jerking his own cock over my still spread pussy.

I have absolutely no idea when he got it out, or whether or not he's been similarly stroking himself all this time, but by God he's far gone. His cock's even slicker than Brandon's, and somehow it's bigger, too – with a swollen tip that looks fit to burst. A little pulsing aftershock goes through me to see it, and the pulse gets stronger when I see how copiously he's leaking pre-come.

It's all down his working fist and, as I watch, a bead of it wells in the slit to join the rest of the mess. It makes me want to lean forwards and lick, to take him in my mouth just as I had imagined, but the moment I get up the balls to actually do it his entire body jerks, and that impossible swollen head swells even further, and a burst of fluid erupts from the tip.

Unlike Brandon, he isn't exactly quiet about it.

'Ohhhhh fuuccck yeah, ohhhh, Jesus, I'm coming, I'm coming. Baby, you're so fucking hot, ohhhh yeah. Oh yeah that's it, that's it, spread yourself. Spread it, let me come on your clit.'

Which I do, gladly. I do it before he even mentions it, eager to feel that hot wet liquid against my still aching bud. And once he's finished coating me in his copious spend, I can't resist rubbing it into my swollen lips and over the sensitive tip of my clit – though I swear I don't mean to turn it into a masturbatory session in front of my best friends. I just don't want it to stop once I've started, my second orgasm welling up in me as easy as anything.

And I guess it's this that I remember afterwards. Two sets of heated eyes on me, as I circle my clit frantically. Both of them murmuring encouragement through that same unsettling silence we started this whole thing in.

And then finally the pleasure – the most intense pleasure of my entire life – courtesy of an experience we never repeat again.

Chapter Two

There are lots of things that go through my head when I enter the bar. But my head tries to bypass all of them, for some reason, and just focus on the most inane of the lot: I shouldn't have brought this potted plant. It's a stupid, stupid gift to give two old friends when they've done something as monumental as create this beautiful, incredible place.

It's dark, but I can make out all the little touches that are uniquely them – a gaudy jukebox crouched in the corner, amidst leather so thick and luxurious I can smell it, before I've even managed to perch my ridiculous gift on the bar. There are framed pictures of obscure movies that scream Brandon; dark mahogany that reminds me of Tyler.

It's as though someone smushed them together and somehow made a watering hole, and not only because of the décor. There's a workbench by the door marked STAFF, as sloppy as anything I ever saw Brandon around. And over the back of one the seats by the skating-rink-slick bar there's a suit jacket.

It smells of Tyler – of Scotch and cigars and that stuff he used to wear that cost more than the gross domestic capital of Brazil. Though of course once I realise this, I have to also accept that I just smelled his clothes.

Five years, and I just *smelled* his *clothes*. Lord only knows what I'll do when I see either or both of them. Blurt out something embarrassing about threesomes, most likely, and then never dare to show my face around them again.

Like I did last time.

'Maisie!' someone cries from the front door I definitely shouldn't have put my back to. I can't let either of them catch me unawares ever again, and yet somehow I've already done just that.

Brandon is on me before I've even worked up the wherewithal to turn around. And he doesn't do anything half-hearted, either, like pat me on the arm or offer me an awkward smile. He actually loops one arm around my shoulders from behind, in a way that's so reminiscent of The Thing We Did I almost gasp. It's like having a bucket of cold water dumped over my head – if a dumped bucket of cold water was one of my kinks, and having it done left my vagina in a quivering state of arousal.

'I can't believe you came,' Brandon says, but I understand where he's coming from. I can't believe it, either. I spent all day yesterday thinking about what a bad idea this was, and now I'm here I know one thing with a deathly certainty: it's a hundred times worse than my wildest imaginings. My entire body has clenched so hard I can't even turn around and greet him properly, and the feeling gets stronger when he finally makes his way to my front.

He looks exactly as I remember, right down to the backwards baseball cap and the hunched shoulders and, oh, that kinking-sideways grin. 'It's like you're a robot from the future who's trying to simulate a smile,' I used to tell him.

Back when I dared to do things like that.

Now I just stand here and stare at his stupidly handsome face, head full of ridiculous thoughts like: *Were his arms really that big before?* And, *Oh Lord, you could cut your finger on that jawline of his.*

Because you could, you really could. Up this close he's almost unbearably handsome, and apparently I'm not responding to that very well. The clenched feeling has gone, but it's been replaced by a prickling under my arms and a heavy sensation low down in my gut, like maybe he punched me when I wasn't looking.

14

I want to double over, quick, before this staring contest gets any weirder.

'It's totally awesome to see you,' he says, but as he does so he puts both hands in his pockets. Those shoulders bunch together even more tightly, and even if I didn't know him I'd understand what that means.

It isn't totally awesome to see me, at all. I'm a relic of his odd threesome-having past, thrown up on the beach of this bar. This place that now looks more and more like a cocoon they've both wrapped themselves in so that they don't have to face the kind of people they once were.

Brandon – goofy and too sweet. Tyler ... oh God, Tyler.

I'm wrong, I'm wrong about Tyler. He *can* face himself.

When he emerges from behind the staff door he looks so eminently confident in who he is, so flawless and be-suited, that for a moment I can't look directly at him. I have to gaze somewhere just north of his right shoulder and hope for the best.

'Here she is,' he says, and I find myself wondering: Was his voice like this before? And if it was, how on earth did I bear it on a daily basis? It just pours out of his mouth like melting chocolate, and before I know where I am the stuff is up to my inner thighs.

I'm not going to come out of this alive, I know.

'God, you look good,' he tells me, as he glides around

the end of the bar, arms outstretched. And then I realise – he's not signalling to some imaginary plane that's flying in, he's moving towards me like that because he actually expects me to hug him. Front to front, too, and not just the little half-cocked one-armed thing Brandon attempted.

I can't, I think, *I can't*, but by the time I've finished resisting in my head I've been engulfed. The scent from the suit jacket surrounds me, deeply familiar and almost too much to bear, but it's the feel of his body that really pushes me over the edge. The shirt he's wearing is strangely flimsy, and I swear I feel the burr of his chest hair against my cheek. I feel his heavy flesh pushing against various pressure points on my body: the tips of my tits, suddenly sensitive; my lips, which I didn't actually mean to part when he pulled me in.

Now I'm practically kissing his left pec, and, oh, that muscle is so damned heavy. It's so solid. I think I might be wet between my legs, over nothing more than some brief hugs and a generous compliment.

'Doesn't she look good, Bran?' he asks, but he's talking out of his ass. I'm wearing jeans and my hair's all loosely pulled back in a way that suggests I'm about to wash my face, and both things look singularly incongruous in a place like this. I need a cocktail dress, I need high heels, I need Prada.

I need some goddamn steel plating.

'Yeah,' Brandon replies, but he seems about as

convinced as I am. There's this expression on his face that I don't recognise – a sort of uncomfortable, half-pained look – and it gets tighter and more intense as this goes on.

By the time we've gotten around to talking about tonight, he's almost beside himself – though I've no idea why. Is he really this bothered by how I look, five years later? I feel like telling him: people age, you know. And also, sometimes they just want to wear their comfortable trainers and an old jersey. Not everyone can be as awesome and Calvin Klein as you, jockstrap.

All of which is a little unkind, I know, but sue me. I'm caught in a mahogany cage, and I'm vulnerable.

'So, are you staying in town?' Tyler asks, and of course he does so at exactly the wrong time. It's just after I've noticed that Brandon seems overpoweringly eager to get away, and right before he makes this sound: *hurk*.

So I don't think I can be blamed for my response, exactly. 'Oh … no. No, I just thought I'd … you know, stop in and say congratulations. I mean, I have this hair appointment, and I've got to call at the dry cleaner's before it closes, so …'

There's no hair appointment. And I'll be perfectly honest, I don't even own any clothes that need dry cleaning.

'I should probably just get going.'

Of course I think of the note I left for them both the

moment I've said it. The similarities are uncanny, they really are – the same awkward excuses about having to do something that doesn't exist, the same vague end to it. I mean, could I have crammed more non-specific hedging in there? All I need are some *littles* and *maybes* to go with those *reallys* and *justs*, and we're right back to where we left off.

It's like it hasn't been five years, at all. It's been five seconds.

'Seriously? You're going to skip the party?'

Such an elegant choice of words from him, truly. *Skip* instead of anything less loaded, like *not able to make* or maybe even *miss*. Skip suggests I'm running out on them; that I'm a flake who can't hold my shit together – and I'm pretty sure he knows that.

The years have only made him stronger, smoother, better. I bet he could talk Mother Teresa into a gangbang with very little effort at all. Despite the fact that she's been dead for God knows how long.

'Well, I'm really not dressed for a –' I start, but he anticipates that, too. He anticipates it before I've even finished talking, and he does it in a way that makes me simultaneously angry and ready to faint on a chaise longue.

'Here, take my credit card. Get yourself something,' he says, just like that. As though he's James Bond or Aristotle Onassis or some other smooth sort of character that I can't even think of, because seriously no one is like this. And it's not just me that thinks so because once the offer is made Brandon gives him such a look.

I think he actually starts to tell him *don't*, too, but after another shared and silent exchange that I'm not a part of, Brandon glances away, defeated. And all of Tyler's three-hundred-watt attention is back on me again.

'Of course, I think you look fine as you are,' he says, and I wonder if it's in response to that expression of Brandon's. Like maybe he was teasing me and Brandon knew it, and now that the look has been exchanged he's changing tack.

Or at least, I imagine something like that until his gaze slides over me, inch by inch, and that chocolate-box voice drops an octave lower.

'That jersey is very ...' he starts, but I'm just left to imagine the rest.

Tight, I think, he wants to say *tight*. If that's true it only leaves me with one option: he really is staring at my tits. Oh Lord, I think he's actually staring at my tits, and it's making my face red and my body go all hot and cold, to the point where I'm actually relieved when Brandon blurts out: 'OK, well, if she can't stay for the party she can't stay for the party. Nothing to do about that! Oh, by the way, Ty, I really need to talk to you in the back about some ... thing.'

Even if those ramblings kind of sound like he hates me.

'Yeah, really, guys, you go ahead and talk about your … thing. I'm just going to head back,' I say, and I swear, I come *this* close to escape. This close, before Tyler runs a hand around my shoulders and leans in far too close, to murmur in my ear.

'Oh no, we wouldn't hear of it,' he tells me, while my spine turns to jelly and slides right out of my body. I know what's going to happen here, before it actually does. 'You just take my credit card and see Marie at Ebe, she'll take care of you. And then when you come back we can all have a real talk, about old times. What do you say?'

I say a million different things, in my head – mostly about how smoothly arrogant he now seems, and how awkward this all is, and how bizarrely aroused I feel. But, of course, I don't voice any of them. It's impossible to voice any of them when Tyler's practically kissing the side of my face and Brandon's looking at me with these big, kind of shocked eyes.

So instead I just go with the safest option: 'OK.'

* * *

I think, in all honesty, that I intend to get in my car and drive back to Hollingdale without a second thought. And yet somehow I find myself going to this annoyingly pretentious boutique Tyler mentioned, and, sure enough a woman called Marie does help me out – as though he's done this a thousand times before for a million different women, and all of them fit into these tiny, drafty clothes far better than I do.

I have to come away with a dress that's more akin to a jumper, in truth, because everything makes me look like some obscene whore of Babylon. And as I drive back to the bar I can't help wondering if he knew that. He knew everything would cling to my enormous breasts and skim somewhere just shy of my vagina. He knew, and sent me there anyway like some more terrible version of *Pretty Woman*.

I can hardly bring myself to walk back into the bar, and not just because of the sluttish glimpse I catch of myself in the slick black exterior. The place is packed, and pushing through the crowd in a dress that's continually threatening to show my gauche panties is not a fun time for me.

Someone fondles my ass, I think – though it could just as easily be a wayward bar stool, brushing against me in the dark. I'm so oversensitised and on the edge of God knows what that I can't tell the difference, and by the time I get over to the table of honour I think it's showing.

My face is flushed, my hair is in disarray and, worst of all, my nipples are stiff and poking through the material. I know they are, without looking, because every single move I make flags it up and, even if it didn't, Tyler's eyes immediately shift downwards to the offending articles.

I want to die. Oh God, please just let me die. I'm sorry for what I said earlier, about wanting to get through this alive. I don't at all.

'Maisie!' Tyler says, and I can tell he's had a couple. Not enough to make him drunk, of course, but he's relaxed back against the booth he's in, and he's spread both his arms around the girls on either side of him.

Plus he's just shouted my name. There's a clue, right there.

'Have a seat,' he tells me, but here's the thing: there's not a seat *to* have. The whole horseshoe shape of the booth has been filled with people I don't know at all, right down to my once-were-best-friends, Brandon and Tyler. They're just as unfamiliar as anything else in this place, now that the former's got a beer and the latter's got a Scotch, and they're both just staring at me in equally uncomfortable ways.

Tyler looks as though he'd like to hunt me down, on the Serengeti. Brandon looks as though I just sprouted a third arm, and am about to batter him with it.

'Oh no, really – there's not room,' I manage, but it's hard to, with those dark eyes trained resolutely on the side of my face. I can tell without glancing at him that he wants to check out what Tyler's obviously checking out, but Brandon was never like that. He'd never just go for anything.

Tyler had to do it for him, always.

'Sure there is,' Tyler says, before adding the very worst thing he possibly could. Worse than *Suck my cock*, worse than *Get those clothes off* – because of course, I could get out of orders like those. I'd be completely justified in slapping his handsome face, the moment he said them to me.

But I can't get out of: 'Just sit in Brandon's lap.'

It's just too innocent, out there on its own, devoid of consequences. All of these staring, giggling girls would think I was an absolute maniac if I acted offended over so slight a thing. One of them is practically in Brandon's lap, as it is, and she has to vacate when I fumble my way over to him.

And, oh, she gives me such a look as I sit down. Clearly, she was happy where she was, with one leg hooked over Brandon's and one boob almost in his face. I want to tell her that we can trade back if she wants. I'll sit where she is, next to a guy whose name turns out to be Patrick, and she can make Brandon incredibly uncomfortable to her heart's content.

Because he obviously is – uncomfortable, I mean. I try to perch on the very edges of his knees, but I can feel how rigid he's gone, even so. And though he seems determined to put his hands somewhere normal – like maybe on my waist or my thighs – he can't bring himself to do it. Those hands hover around one place and then

23

another, never quite settling, before they finally find their place somewhere weird.

Like behind his head.

Without even glancing back, I know how he'll look. He's turned himself into a tourist, relaxing on an imaginary beach. All he needs is a parasol and a book and none of this will seem insane at all.

'You OK?' he asks, which probably means he's sensed the tension I'm using to keep myself like this. I'm almost holding myself in a sitting position, without anything under me to sit on. It's like doing a series of really, really awful squats, only I don't get to relax at the end of each one. I just have to keep going and going, until I faint.

'Great,' I tell him, though my treacherous voice belies that one word. It comes out all wavering and near to exhaustion, until he simply has to say. He has to. He wouldn't be the gentleman I remember, if he didn't.

'You know, you can sit back a little, if you want,' he offers, but he doesn't shout the words over the thrum of all this noise. He slides them underneath, low and furtive, and when I shove myself back into the welcoming curve of his body I understand why.

He's hard.

He's so hard that he actually makes a little sound when I push into him, and tries to shove me forwards again. Like if he does it fast enough, I won't notice his hugely stiff cock. I won't remember exactly how it felt, rubbing up against me. I'll just continue not listening to the conversation around the table, oblivious and innocent.

Though I think he knows, on some level, that this won't wash. I can feel how tense he's gone, and those hands are now iron in the hollows of my hips. Any move on my part and they clamp down tight, like a warning: *Do not take this any further. Do not pass go, do not collect two hundred pounds, do not turn around and look at me in that way.*

But he's out of luck on the third thing. I have to turn around and look, I *have* to. What expression goes with *sudden erection*? And how different is it from the ones he levelled at me earlier, which mostly seemed to be about getting away from me, as fast as possible?

The answer is: not that different at all. He's still got that touch of pain around his ever-square and too-tight mouth, and he won't meet my gaze. He just does what I did earlier – fixes his eyes on some point just north of my shoulder, and hopes for the best.

But I can't give him what he wants. I can't be the way I was before, passive and silent and sort of unsure. That girl hadn't lived through five years of boyfriends falling asleep on top of her, and endless nights with nothing but a vibrator for company. She didn't understand what it's like to regret a missed opportunity, but I do.

And I want to rub myself against the thick, stiff shape of his cock, until I hear him moan. Oh God, he *moans* – and not even in a quiet sort of way, either. It just blurts out of him like a short sharp shock, and once it's done I think we both know we're in trouble.

I glance up and, sure enough, Tyler is looking our way. And though his expression is mainly amused, there's something else there, too, buried deep down in that foggy gaze of his. It's a look I recognise – a look I've seen a million times before, without fully understanding what it meant.

But I understand now.

Ohhhh, yeah. I understand now. He wants to fuck me I think, blindly, and once the idea is there I can't shake it off. It gets a hold of me between my legs, and forces me to do things I wouldn't usually. I'm sure I'd just leave it at a little light rubbing if I were left to my own devices.

But once Tyler's got his lust-fucked gaze on me I find myself doing much worse. I actually ease myself back and forth over Brandon's solid prick and, when he protests – when he gasps and digs his fingers into the hollows of my hips – I put an arm around his shoulder.

So that my breasts are almost pressed against his face.

'Maisie,' he says, but he sends the word high and wild. And his efforts at following it with something saner – something like *please stop*, maybe – don't quite pan out for him. Instead he ends up turning until his mouth is very close to my mouth and his hands are very close to holding me, and, after a moment of this delicious tension,

I think: *We're going to kiss.* That's what this is: the leaning into one another, and his hand suddenly on the nape of my neck. He wants to kiss me, but something's holding him back – perhaps Tyler's gaze burning across the table at us, too intense for me to fully process.

I can't even look at him directly without assuming what Brandon probably does – that it's anger, or jealousy, or something else similarly crazy that he's levelling at us. And I think this until the point where I actually do meet his eyes and see for myself what he's saying.

It's not stop. It's go. *Go on,* he says to me with his smouldering stare. *Go on, kiss him. Touch him. Fuck him right here on this table until you're wrung out and slippery with your own come and his spunk …* Oh God, how can one look be so filthy? How can it make me so crazy?

Because it does. The feel of Brandon's stiff cock – now almost in the groove between the cheeks of my arse, rubbing and rutting insistently – is bad enough. The tension of this almost-kiss, so hot and slick, is bad enough.

But Tyler's gaze makes me weaker. My nipples stiffen under the weight of it. My sex grows full and fat, every bit of pressure against it suddenly maddening. I want to rub just to relieve that sensation, I realise – maybe spread my legs over one of his thighs and get my clit right up against that meaty muscle – but I don't get the chance to.

A moment later, Brandon shifts all in a big rush, some unearthly sound bubbling out of him as he does. And though I'm sure he means to be careful he isn't – his hands turn rough on my body, manhandling me in a way that's simultaneously exciting and disheartening. Exciting because there's a new urgency to the move that I can't deny. Disheartening because once he's done, I'm left sprawled on the seat, while he blunders off in the direction of the door marked STAFF.

In his defence, he does offer me a few blurted words before leaving. Something about the bathroom and needing it, and that he'll be back in a minute – probably sans erection.

But, unfortunately for him, I don't feel like letting him reset the clock. It's already been done once, and once was enough. Now it's time for seizing the day, rattling the cages, feeding the thing that's grown inside me over five years of wondering, What if?

What if I hadn't left, without a goodbye?

What if I'd gotten up off my seat, pushed through the crowd and gone through the door marked STAFF, to see what was on the other side?

Chapter Three

'Oh Maisie, come on. Give me a break,' he says the second I uncover him, hiding in some storage room at the back of this place. I understand why, however. He looks like some wild, slightly insane version of himself. His hair is standing on end from what I can only imagine were a million hand-strokes through it, and somewhere along the way he's lost his suit jacket.

The one that Tyler probably picked out for him in some fancy shop. I can almost see the scenario in my mind's eye: Brandon squirming inside material too expensive for him; Tyler straightening out the collar, in firm, sort of … brisk movements.

Like the kind of movements he used on my body when I lay naked in front of him.

'A break from what?' I ask, but I'm not being fair here, and I know it. It's obvious what he needs a breather from, all things considered. And by all things considered, I mean I rubbed my ass against his cock, while his best friend watched.

'Just …' he starts, only there's no finish. His hands make frustrated patterns in the air, instead, before returning to that crazy hair.

And then I'm just left to interpret this new form of sign language.

Which I do. In the worst possible way I can.

'You want me to not touch your cock?' I say, only this time my faux-innocence has a little bonus on the end. It features the word 'cock', and the word 'cock' has rather unexpected side effects. It sends a bolt of heat, right through me. It strokes a slow, slick hand between my legs. And, best of all, it turns his face the colour of a ripe tomato – like he's embarrassed, I think. I've backed him into a corner, and now our roles from before are near reversed.

Though I've no idea how or when that happened.

'Because I can stop touching it any time you like,' I say, in a voice that doesn't belong to me. It belongs to my aching, swollen cunt, and apparently she wants it to be low, soft, persuasive.

'Did you … did you talk to Tyler about this?' he asks, which almost gives me pause.

I think of the strange way they'd operated before. How silent things had seemed. How unspoken. But then the feeling passes, and this is what I'm left with: the firm swell of Brandon's cock beneath my palm.

'No. Why?'

'Oh, so you're just … doing that. OK. OK. Do you … maybe think we should have a conversation first? Like, we could go to dinner and after dinner I could walk you home and then … Ohhhhh Jesus, really?'

I can't help drawing a red circle around several of the things he's said: dinner, conversation, *ohhhh Jesus*. And I draw a circle around the actions that go with the words too: the way his hand snaps down to stop mine; the up-on-tiptoe move he makes, automatically, as though the feel of the heel of my palm against his stiff dick is more akin to being attacked with a cattle prod.

But that's fine. I want him to be zinged. I was zinged, five years ago – this feels like some sort of mad revenge. Or maybe it's a mad reward for all of my waiting and wanting and running away. Now I get to fondle his solid prick through his trousers until he stops resisting and starts begging me for more.

'Yeah, just like that,' he tells me, because I've found the ridge around the head of his cock, and when I rub just so – back and forth with my thumb, through the material – he trembles for me. He bucks into my palm and puts a hand on my shoulder, more words spilling out of him, one after the other.

'Kiss me,' he says. 'Kiss me.'

But I don't want to kiss. I want to finally and properly know what his cock looks like, and feels like, and, more importantly, tastes like. And since he seems intent on letting me do whatever the fuck I want, it's not that hard to do. I just ease his stiff length out into the open, while he hums like someone set his internal motor going.

'Are you really going to …' he says.

I have no idea why he is doubting. Anyone would want to suck a cock like his – so smooth and silky and stiff, with a curve to it that suggests just the right sort of angle for hitting all those good spots.

And he's practically dripping by this point, too. I rub the pad of my thumb over the head and I can feel all of that delicious pre-come sliding around in a way that makes us both moan – though he doesn't break until I'm on my knees. He doesn't give me the words, until I've got the head of his cock in my mouth and my tongue is working and working over that slippery slit.

And then he just lets it out.

'God, yeah, give it to me, Maisie,' he says, so I do. I eat at him hungrily, sloppily, until the entire head of his cock is as glossy as I am between my legs. And when that doesn't seem like enough to sate either me or him, I use my hands. I rub his stiff length roughly, finishing each stroke with a lick or a suck that gets him gasping.

He's going to come soon, I can tell. I can feel it before he tells me – *Oh, honey, you're going to make me do it* – in the tightness of his balls and the swell of his cock. And I want it, I really want it, over what I got last time: come striping my skin, almost independent of anything I had done.

And I want to watch him, too, while he does it.

Though in my defence, it's hard not to crave something like that. He seems to have forgotten how to breathe, and every time I switch to something new – like a little flick over that sensitive spot, just under the head, or a squeeze of his impossibly tight balls – he tries to let some air out. Or let some air in. Or just do something, anything besides biting his lip and straining towards my hot, wet mouth.

It's an oddly arousing thing to observe. Like I'm seeing myself five years ago, caught between *I really want to* and *I kind of shouldn't* – which of course makes me wonder why he is. Why is he letting me do this, after his odd reaction earlier? And in this storeroom, of all places, where anyone could walk in and find us. I mean it's not as though the door's locked, and even if it was there's always someone who'll have the key.

Like Tyler, for instance.

Tyler, who I'm barely aware of until Brandon jerks and tries to cover himself. Then afterwards I'm very aware of him, because not only is Brandon trying to pretend he didn't know this might happen, but Tyler has his hand on the back of my head. I can feel it, even when I'd like to think it's something else altogether. Maybe Brandon sprouted a third hand when I wasn't looking and now he's urging me to suck his cock, even as he tells me not to.

'Oh my God no,' he says, and I hear rather than see him clang back against the kegs. He's trying to get away, I think, but in all honesty if he is, he's not doing a very good job of it.

Or is it just that Tyler's now applying a bit of pressure? A very specific sort of pressure, I might add, that fills my mouth with cock even as Brandon succeeds in squirming backwards. And though I know I should stop if he wants me to, I find I can't.

It's too arousing. Just as before, the excitement thrumming through my body takes over sense, and I do what he's urging me to. I take as much of that still unbearably stiff prick into my mouth as I can and suck with all the enthusiasm I can muster and, when he actually speaks, my brain dissolves and disappears into my vagina.

'Yeah, that good, baby?' he asks. 'Take that cock.'

Lord, I don't think I want to know what Brandon makes of that. I've got my eyes closed, now, because eyes closed is better, but I can feel him starting to really shake. It's not even just a shake, in all honesty, it's more like a prolonged and uncontrollable spasm, and he finishes each jerking motion with a sound.

One that joins Tyler's words in that slippery place between my legs.

'How does she feel?' Tyler asks, but I think he might have gone crazy. If his presence and his hand on my head weren't enough, clue-wise, then his expectation that Brandon's going to answer him surely is. Brandon can't even seem to push him away – though I think he wants to – and when I dare to look his expression is … I don't know.

Furious? Frustrated?

At the very least it's the kind of look that doesn't go with: 'Ohhh, she's so hot. She sucks so hard.'

Though it's true. I do suck hard. It's like I'm trying to lose myself in the feel and taste of him so I don't have to think about anything else: Tyler's insistence and Brandon's reluctance; my own arousal in spite of both these things – or maybe because of them. Every time they say a word, my clit swells and orgasm threatens, even if the word is just: 'Yeah.'

Or: 'God, I'm gonna come.'

Though in all fairness to me, that last one's a bit of no-brainer. I'm actually quite surprised *I* don't come when I feel the first slick spurt of cream over my tongue. And

I'm even more surprised after Tyler's hand tightens in my hair, like a prompt.

Swallow, I think, and then this hot shivery sensation just wriggles through my body. It gets a hold of my cunt and squeezes, and squeezes, until I nearly reach that state of perfect mindlessness. I hardly think of anything at all when I get that first taste of him, filling my mouth, and the feel of his cock swelling and jerking against my tongue.

And the way he moans, too ... Ohhhh yeah. Yeah, I wish I could frame that sound and hang it on my bedroom wall.

As does Tyler, apparently.

'Well, it seems you appreciated that,' he says and, as he does, that hand disappears from the back of my head. I don't know what I feel about that. It's sort of like a relief, but sort of not – and I'm right to react that way.

Because he follows up those words with this: 'Why don't you show her that appreciation with the kiss you were asking for earlier on?'

I immediately wonder how he knows about that – he wasn't even here when Brandon asked. But the wondering doesn't lead anywhere good. It just makes me imagine him stood outside the door, listening for the very best moment to enter and encourage some filthily delicious things.

Which is almost as bad for my libido as Brandon leaning

down to obey. Oh God, he actually obeys. I don't even have time to properly swallow or maybe turn my head – you know, out of politeness – before his lips are pressing wetly to mine. And though I think he tries to get away with something chaste, Tyler's not having any of it.

'What are you waiting for?' he asks, like the dirtiest goad ever, all wrapped up in an innocent package. 'Come on. Give her a real kiss.'

He could be someone's uncle at a wedding, encouraging a nervous groom. Even if Brandon doesn't seem the least bit nervous now. He seems like he did before – all greedy and shaky and totally willing to fuck my mouth with his tongue. In fact, he goes one worse than that and kind of gropes one of my tits as he does it.

Like he knows just what I need.

I need him to be as dirty as he can possibly be in order to reach that higher state of who gives a fuck. I need to know he can taste his own come without flinching, and that he doesn't give a shit what Tyler's doing, or saying. Despite the fact that Tyler is saying, 'Yeah, that's good, right? The taste of yourself, in her mouth. Knowing that you've just fucked her there and filled her with your jizz.'

Which even I find a little strong. And by strong I mean: my cunt clenches to hear him use that word, that one filthy word as though he's not Tyler at all. He's some dirty fucker who wants to push things as far as they will go – to the point where I find myself dancing between fear and anticipation. When Brandon breaks the kiss I turn my head and I can see how hard Tyler is. He's thicker than Brandon, meatier, and it's more obvious through his trousers. Especially when he cups the whole thing one-handed, as he looks down on me with that soft, sleepy gaze of his. It's almost like a prompt – like earlier, in the bar. Him telling me *Go on, go on and do it* with his eyes, until I'm almost reckless, rather than the person I really am.

But this time when I do as he's suggested, he doesn't react as I expect. My head's full of him yanking up my dress and bending me over something, but apparently he is more chaste than I give him credit for. He even puts a hand out to stop me before I reach for the zipper on his trousers, and gives me an unbearably sweet, 'Don't I get a kiss, too?'

Like the Hallmark version of what I'd thought of a moment earlier – one of them getting a turn, then the other, so as not to leave anyone out. They could probably write a really nice kids' story about us: 'My Two Boyfriends Like to Share'.

Despite what Tyler adds, before I manage to climb to my feet.

'Wait,' he says, just as I'm halfway up. And, humiliatingly, I stay like that. He gives me the word and I just hover, half-crouched, waiting for him to give me further instructions.

'Clean him, first. You know how much I abhor a mess, Maisie.'

For a moment I can't believe he's serious. He wants me to … to basically suck Brandon's cock until I've removed every trace of the glistening come I can still see all over it, and then once I'm done he wants me to … well.

Let's be honest, here – he wants to taste whatever I've cleaned up. I can see it in his face and actually hear it in his words, and even if I couldn't it's definitely in the gasp Brandon gives. The little aroused gasp, which makes his cock twitch and his face heat all over again.

Which is yet another response I'll have to file away for later head-discussion. Seriously, what's going on here? And why on earth am I just doing it all? Because I totally am. I barely hesitate over his words. I can't – they're too casual and too exciting and besides, they mostly mean I get to taste Brandon's cock again.

And then I get to stand up on legs that won't hold me and feel Tyler sliding a steadying hand around my waist. Just like that – so smooth and confident and knowing. He gets that I can't keep this up on my own. He understands how raw I'm feeling and how aroused.

And he wants to reward me with some support, before he takes my mouth.

Because, oh, he does. He doesn't kiss like Brandon, a little hesitant, a lot greedy. He kisses like my mouth is my pussy, and he wants me to feel every last drop of pleasure he can possibly squeeze out of it. His mouth works over mine, firm and sure, that thick slippery tongue of his finding sensitive spots I didn't even know existed.

My upper lip is a fist of nerve endings, apparently, and they all fire at once when he pulls back a little and catches it with this little spiky lick. And the way he holds me … that hand on my waist, the other on the back of my head. I could almost go to sleep in his arms, they're so solid. He's such a … a *professional*.

Though, of course, underneath this veneer is the suggestion he made a second ago: that he's not just kissing me in a romantic end-of-the-movie sort of way.

He's kissing me so he can taste Brandon's come. And he's doing it so thoroughly that I don't think I'm mad to suspect that's the main reason for his behaviour. I mean, maybe there's something between them that I don't know about. Maybe Tyler has a Big Secret he's afraid of sharing.

Or maybe he just really, really wants to slide that hand down over my ass, as he groans heavily into my mouth. Yeah, maybe there's that – though I swear I still suspect something. I do. There could be some unresolved tension here, some issues that he doesn't feel he can talk about.

And then he starts fondling my left breast, and after that I'm not sure what I suspect any more. That I'm out of my depth maybe? That I don't know anything about anything? All of these things are true, and remain so when he finally breaks away.

He's still hard, I note. So I guess kissing girls doesn't exactly put him off. Plus, once he's caught his breath, he turns to a frankly dazed Brandon and hands him a set of keys. Tells him to take me upstairs, as though this is a completely different type of movie to the one I've just been contemplating. I was thinking *Guys Get It On 4*.

He's apparently thinking *Slave Girls of the Sultan's Harem*.

With him being the sultan, naturally.

And though that thought should make me bolt, I know, I find I can't. Not again. Not like last time. I'm just not the same person; I'm not willing to live with those regrets; I'm not the kind of girl who can abandon someone twice. And most importantly, of course: I'm so aroused I could die.

Chapter Four

I wake up the sound of whispering, but it's not the first thing I concentrate on. Mostly I just get a blast of how the fuck did I fall asleep, followed by a flick book of memories. Brandon being awkward, showing me around the Spartan little place above the bar, one or both of them apparently owns; bare wooden boards, no curtains on the broad, cold windows; nothing in the fridge, nothing on any available surface.

Nothing to be said.

And then he'd shown me the bed parked in some corner behind a sliding door, and somehow I'd sat down on it. Maybe I'd hoped he was going to join me, in a second – or at least, my vagina had hoped he might. But I guess when he didn't I simply passed out from sheer arousal overload.

It *feels* like that's what happened. I'm still in my clothes for a start. And sometime in the middle of the night my make-up has slid halfway down my face, so I don't think I'm wildly off base.

However, I am focusing on the wrong thing entirely. Nobody cares if my mascara has made comedy telescope circles around my eyes. People aren't interested in my shoes, which seem to have disappeared in the middle of the night.

No, mostly everyone just wants to know what the fuck the men behind me are talking about, at what looks like a bleary six thirty in the morning. And I appease these people. I do. I have to – they're banging on some big gong inside me, marked *Your two old friends are talking about you. Stop checking whether you still have your panties on!*

'I think she's awake.'

'She's not awake. She'd say something if she were.'

That last voice is Tyler's. I can make it out even under cover of darkness, and in a tone best described as *government conspiracy*.

'How do you know? You keep talking like you understand her completely, but you don't. It was five years ago. She's probably … like … a whole different person.'

'You mean like a whole different person who blows you in a store cupboard?'

'Just shut up, all right? Let's go back to the living room.'

'You mean the hovel?'

'Hey, you wanted me to bring her up here. I could have just as easily taken her back to your swanky pad so you could ... pffft.'

Funny, really, that he thinks I must have changed so much, when I know exactly what he means by that little blart of frustrated air. I can translate it exactly: *So you could fuck her.*

'Is that what you want me to do?' Tyler asks, and I can hear it then. The tone has changed. Now he's not vaguely teasing and bullish. He's almost grave, in a way I'm not sure I've heard from him before.

And the silence that follows is similar, before Brandon finally answers. 'No.'

'So what is it you want me to do?' Tyler asks, and that surprises me even more than his change in tone. He'd seemed so smooth and in control the night before, and it had suited him. It had suited him so well that I can't recall how our last encounter played out.

Was Brandon the one who initiated it, or was it Tyler? And if Tyler did, is this what he offered before it? A question, plainly put, that Brandon can't seem to answer? Because by God he can't. I can almost hear him wrestling with it, despite the fact that my back is turned and my head is in the pillow.

I just don't understand either of them. I don't know what their ... what their *goal* is.

Until Tyler spells it out for me. 'You get that she won't say no if you just roll over and slide a hand up her dress.'

He's right, you know. *No* isn't the first thing that springs to mind, when I think of an idea like that. It's not even on the list. It's somewhere below *setting myself on fire* and *gouging out one of my own eyes*, on the page marked things I will never do.

And as for that other stuff he mentioned …

I can't think about it without melting between my legs. All of that excitement comes crashing back to my body in one big glut, and, oh, the heat from it is unbearable. It makes a little electric fire low down in my belly, and every time he says a certain word or phrase – *hand up her skirt* being one of them – the warmth blooms outwards, in a shaky pulse.

I have to bite my lip and squeeze my legs together, just to stop it taking me over altogether. Clearly, it's already consumed them, and after that – then what? The world?

'I'm not doing that.'

'Why not? Go on, give me a good reason.'

'She's asleep.'

'She wasn't asleep last night. You still didn't do anything.'

'It's not that easy, Tyler.'

'She made it seem easy.'

'Because you … you made her.'

'So we're going to go over this again. You know, some people enjoy a little cajoling.'

'It's different when … It's not … I like it, OK? You don't know if she does.'

'True. But I know she was practically too turned on to walk last night, and yet you still didn't do anything. All night long … you've just left her hanging. Does that sound like the actions of a gentleman?'

There's a brief silence and it's far from a comfortable one. I can almost feel the tension flowing from it, and it's not just because I'm holding my breath. I could be drilling a hole in the wall and I'd sense it.

Brandon's voice is different when he finally does speak. 'Don't do this, Tyler,' he says, so sharp and steady you could cut a tin can on that letter T.

Tyler pays no attention, however. 'Don't do what? I'm just saying – she got you off in spectacular fashion, and in return you just watched her fall asleep.'

'I didn't watch her, all right? I came in *once* to check on her!'

Oh *Lord*. He feels so strongly for me that he actually has to protest when someone pulls on that thread? At this point, I honestly don't know what's worse: that Tyler is turning the screws on him like this, or that I'm loving it.

I don't mean to be, but I am. He really does like me, even after all this time. He likes me so much that he doesn't seem to know what to do with himself when Tyler presents the following to him: 'Just think about how wet she must be, right now. Wouldn't you be hard if she'd just wriggled in your lap and rubbed those amazing tits in your face before coming up here for a nap? You're hard now and she hasn't even done anything but lie there.'

'*You're* doing something,' Brandon spits back, sullen now.

It's not the sullenness I'm concentrating on, however. It's those words he used, oh good Lord those words – what does he mean? Does he just mean that Tyler's talking is driving him up the wall, or …

'You want me to stop?' Tyler asks, but I think we all know the answer to that. Brandon doesn't even make an attempt at a response. He just carries on in silence, while I eat my own pounding heart out, listening for any little hint of something beyond *chatting*.

I mean, Tyler *did* want to taste him, didn't he? And this is a very close, heated conversation for two just-good-friends to be having. Maybe Tyler's got his hand on something or his mouth near something or Christ, I don't know.

I'm not even sure about threesomes. Throw a little man on man into the mix and I'm lost.

'Or do you want me to carry on talking about what her pussy probably looks like right around now?' Tyler finally, *finally* says, but I don't know whether to be relieved or not. I'm not even sure if relieved is the right word for what I probably should be feeling, because, well … I have no monopoly on them. If they want to do things together, they can.

Though they should probably know that it hugely turns me on when they do the things this close to me.

'Don't,' Brandon says, but now I can tell. He doesn't mean it at all.

'I bet she's soaking wet. Just absolutely drenched. If she turned over and spread her legs right now, you'd probably see it glistening all over her thighs.'

He's not wrong. The squeezing-my-legs together technique isn't really working, because of that very problem. Everything just feels so slippery and messy down there, in a way that's only exacerbating matters.

'Imagine what her spread pussy looks like … all that glossy cream coating her folds and her swollen clit. Because she's got to be swollen by now. You probably wouldn't even need to do very much, to get her off – a little stroke over that stiff bud and she'd be screaming your name.'

'Or yours.'

'Does it matter?'

'I don't know any more, I don't know. Keep going,' Brandon pants, and, oh, those two words. They're almost as good as all the poetry of the pussy Tyler's spouting, though I have trouble figuring out why. I think it's because they suggest Brandon's complicity in this thing – that he knows what it is and wants it, even as he says don't.

Or maybe it's just because he sounds like he's jerking off, while he says it.

'That feel good?'

Oh yeah, he's definitely jerking off.

'Just … carry on.'

'While she's lying right there? Oh, Bran. How can you live with yourself?' Tyler says, and though he's teasing I kind of want to draw the line here. Maybe announce my presence in this conversation, or tell him off in some way. I mean, if Brandon *is* masturbating, I don't see why he should feel bad about that.

Though, of course, worrying about him feeling bad relies on one fairly major assumption: that he does. And, judging by his next reaction, I'm just not sure I've pegged things right.

'Mmm, yeah.'

'She's not a foot from you, you little slut.'

'Oh God, OK, OK.'

'Want me to talk some more about her pussy? Or maybe we could revisit an old favourite – the things that Maisie might possibly like. What do you think? You think she likes to be fingered while you go down on her?'

Oh yes please. Seriously, why aren't I turning over at this point? Is it just fear of Brandon being embarrassed?

Although he seems fine. In fact, it seems like he's humping his hand, if the rocking of the bed is anything to go by.

'Or maybe she'd like something more substantial – fill her with a dildo while you lick her clit … Yeah, that sounds good. Though if we really want to go over old times, you could fill her with something else while *I* lick her clit. What do you say? You want to fuck her while I go down on her?'

I honestly had no idea that Tyler was this good at dirty talk. Really no clue. I mean, I knew he had the confidence, and certainly he didn't hold back when we were together, but he's so refined. His voice is like crushed velvet – though that only seems to make it worse. He's practically reaching across the bed to stroke me with each lewd suggestion, in a way that makes me certain he knows. He just does.

I'm awake, and he's aware of it.

And now he's just waiting for my breaking point.

'Or maybe I could fuck her while you go down on her – yeah, that sounds good, huh? I could pound that tight little pussy of hers while you make a mess of your face. Maybe she'd even suck you while you go at it … What do you think? Think she'd be up for that?'

The answer is yes. Always yes, Tyler. There's just one teeny tiny problem, however: I can't seem to get that word out of my mouth. And, apparently, neither can Brandon.

'I don't know, I don't know,' he moans, despite the fact that he hasn't stopped masturbating. I can actually hear him, now – that slick shuttle of a hand, over a slippery cock, the pacing of his breathing, sometimes tight and sometimes rapid. He's going to come soon, I think, but he shouldn't feel bad about that.

I'm going to come soon and no one's doing anything to me. I'm not even doing anything to myself, except maybe squeezing my thighs together, occasionally. And I'll be perfectly frank – the squeezing is doing absolutely nothing for me. I might as well be punching myself in the face.

'Oh no, wait ... I've got the best one. Yeah, yeah, how about this? You fuck her sweet little pussy and, while you're busy with that, I'll get her ass all nice and slick and then I'll just ease my –'

'Stop! OK, stop, stop, stop. Stop. Just – red rum, OK? No, no, no,' Brandon says, only this time it's obvious he means it – for more than one reason. First off: he practically shouts the words, even though they've been keeping things quiet up till now. Secondly: the rocking of the bed ceases, about a hair's breadth after he's said it.

And finally – most damningly – I'm fairly certain that's a safe word. He just said a safe word to Tyler, over some sexual thing that Tyler is saying, while I'm lying not a foot from him. Because let's be honest here – there aren't many other things those two words could mean in a situation like this.

My two best friends have a safe word. *Together*. For … for what? Situations like this one? And, if that's the case, then is it also the case that situations like this one arise with some *frequency*?

I don't know. I don't know anything about anything. I'm too flabbergasted to process real thoughts or formulate actual questions. My whole body is frozen to the bed in this one curled position, to the point where I'm starting to cramp up and maybe get dry eye from all the wild staring into nothing but my pillow.

God only knows how I'm ever going to move again. Or talk again. Or do anything again that requires me to get up off this bed, go into the living room, sit at that one rickety table and look both of them in the eye.

Because of course when I eventually go through all of those motions, I'll have to say something about this. It's a given, really, and not just due to the fact that a second later Tyler gets up from the bed and disappears. Or that Brandon seems really bothered by all of this, in a way I can't quite grasp.

There's also the knowledge in me that I actually want to find out. I want to, because not only am I curious and almost beside myself with excitement, I'm also not willing to walk away this time – far from it.

I want to stay.

I need to stay.

I need them both, and no amount of fear is going to push me away.

* * *

The falsely bright look all over Brandon's face is ... well, it's not a comfort. I was at the very least hoping for something less gaudy, like maybe a nod or a little wink or perhaps an arm around my shoulder. *Hey buddy*, he could have said, then followed it with a casual manoeuvring of me in the direction of my car.

So you're going back to Hollingdale when? he could have said. And after that everything would have been fine. I could have pretended I haven't desperately missed them and now actually realise how much I need them in my life. He could have pretended he didn't shoot his load down my throat last night, before masturbating to Tyler's kinky suggestions, sometime in the a.m.

But the false smile spoils all that. Or maybe it's just my emotional turmoil that spoils all of that, because once he's wavered that thing at me over his morning coffee I can't help blurting things out. I don't even check if Tyler's around, either. I just go for it, balls to the wall.

'You know, if the things he says makes you uncomfortable, you don't have to do them. I mean, *we* don't have to do them.'

Oh good Lord, what on earth did I just say? That wasn't the plan. Abort! Abort!

'And by that what I mean is that we don't have to do anything – I wasn't assuming, you know? I was just, uh … it's just that he said those things and I … I … uh …'

Somewhere inside me, Tact puts her face in her hands. I think I just did the equivalent of farting in a crowded elevator – or worse. Maybe I farted at a funeral, because by God he looks mortified. His face has locked in one position – stone-like horror – and it's only then that I realise the size of what I've done wrong here.

I've started with the assumption that he knows I heard him talking.

When of course he *does not*.

Let's just underline that, shall we: *he does not*.

That was just me, making things up, inside my stupid head.

'You heard that?'

Tact is so lucky. She gets to put her face in her hands without anyone seeing – whereas I have to make do with gripping one of the chairs in front of me very, very tightly, while all my insides freefall through my body and make a home in my feet.

'Let's say I heard a little bit of it,' I try, but the stone horror doesn't leave his face. And then I just go ahead and make it worse – why not! I've already fucked my entire life in the ass with a shotgun. Last week I spent seven hours watching *Homes Under the Hammer*. Things couldn't get much worse. 'I mean, you were lying right next to me.'

'I thought you were asleep.'

'I was. Until you started talking about ... vaginas. And then I woke up.'

I really wish I hadn't used the word 'vagina', there. I don't even know why I did, in truth, because it doesn't make the whole sentence seem less filthy. If anything it just makes it sound as though I'm simultaneously mocking him and trying to turn him on.

Which, I swear, is not my goal. I swear it's not. Even in all the places where it is.

'Oh my God. You heard all of that. You heard ... did you hear Tyler saying that stuff? Oh my God, Maisie, I don't know what you must think, by this point. Look, that stuff in the storage space ... that wasn't my idea. We didn't plan any of this, or had ... you know ... conversations about stuff before you got here. It's just that when you came in, wearing that dress and –'

'No, no, Bran. It's cool. It's OK. I know you didn't plan any of that. I mean, I came on to you.'

He nods like I've just offered him a rope as he slowly sinks into a pit of scorpions and acid. Unfortunately for him, however, said rope has some stuff on the end of it that he's not going to want – killer bees, maybe.

Thinly veiled accusations, perhaps.

'And besides ... it's not like you've *ever* planned to do anything to me. Right?' I say, and then I just wait for his expression to tell me the whole tale. Which it does almost immediately. Of course it does.

He's in a pit of scorpions, acid and killer bees – hiding secrets is the last thing on his mind.

'Well ...' he says, and I get a flash of memory. Both of them sat on the couch, waiting for me to return from the kitchen. Both of them looking as nonchalant as it's possible to look, after just having a conversation about maybe doing me. 'We kind of talked about stuff, before.'

'I see.'

'Back in college.'

'Right.'

'Just about ... you know, how much we liked you.'

'And maybe how hard you'd double-team me, if you got the chance?' I venture, but it's the wrong move. It sounds like I'm offended, and Brandon is certainly offended, and it takes him about half an hour to stop choking on his coffee and answer my increasingly impatient questions.

'No! No. Mainly Tyler just ... I don't know ... suggested how I might go about ... seducing you.'

'Is that what you wanted to do? Seduce me?'

I don't know why I'm so surprised. He did come all over me the last time we were together ... And yet it's still there – that odd feeling I always had of being stuck behind a line marked friendship. We were just friends, we were friends, all right? Nothing more.

We couldn't be anything more, because he was gorgeous and I was not. Because Tyler was gorgeous and I was not. God, I've always felt like *not*.

'Yes.'

'Well, where's the big deal in that?' I ask, and as I do I take the seat opposite him. I stop clutching and barely breathing and being shocked, and just relax into whatever this is going to be. The Conversation, I suppose – though I doubt this variation on that theme is present in many dating guides.

Tell your man what your expectations are, and then listen to him divulging his secret horny chats with your other best friend about threesomes.

'I think you know what the big deal is in that,' he says, and he's right. I just heard the big deal about half an hour ago.

'You mean because a lot of Tyler's seduction tips are horrendously graphic and extremely lewd? Yeah, I kind of got a clue about that.'

He puts a hand over his eyes. 'Oh, man. Did you really hear everything?'

'Like I said, I was a foot from you. And you –'

'I honestly thought you were asleep.'

'Or maybe you wanted me to hear.'

'No. No.'

'I mean, there was a lot of stuff in that discussion that I kind of need to know.'

He shakes his head behind the hand-mask. Hunches his shoulders to the point where he's almost disappearing under the table.

'Like, how much you'd like to fuck me, while Tyler goes down on me,' I say, but I make my voice as playful as I can for it. I'm almost into singsong by the time he interrupts.

'No, I really –'

'Or, maybe some other stuff. About why you and Tyler have a safe word …' I say, and this time I really am into singsong. It doesn't seem to make it any easier on him, however – far from it.

His hand snaps down from his face the second I've spelled it out for him, and his eyes are wide and wild.

'We don't … that's not –' he tries, but he can't seem to manoeuvre around his own high breaths to get the words out. I have to tell him to just take a second, before he can do anything but panic. 'OK. OK. Maybe we have some kind of safe word. But we don't do things together, if that's what you're thinking.'

I shrug before I've even thought about it, though there are other responses simmering away inside me. A faint sense of loss or jealousy maybe, followed by something else I don't really want to consider.

I believe it's called: having voyeuristic tendencies.

'Would it be such a bad thing if you did?'

He shrugs back at me in a way that's not like a shrug at all. Really it's more akin to a tensing of his entire body. 'No.'

'And is it such a bad thing if you talked about having sex with me?' I ask, expecting another half-sure agreement. This time, however, he's a little more ... vociferous. He actually stops twisting his hands together, and makes gestures in the air.

'I just don't want you to think we're assholes, OK? We're not assholes who sit around blabbing about your ass or ... doing things to your ass ... Christ. I can't believe he said that.' He shakes his head, with what looks like just a touch of rue. Yeah, he's mad at Tyler, all right. But I think he's also kind of ... I don't know ... fond of his behaviour? Pleased that things go that way, even if he sort of wants to resist?

Maybe. Maybe.

'He does it a lot, huh? Saying things, I mean,' I offer, and then I wait with bated breath. Truthfully, I'm not sure my breath has been anything but for the last two hours.

'Yeah. Not as much any more. He used to, back in college.' He glances up from beneath those impossibly long lashes – maybe to judge how exactly I feel about this. And when I give him nothing but the stupidly eager expression I know is painted on my face, he plunges on.

'God, he used to drive me up the wall with talk of you. Of the things I should do or say or …'

'Or what?'

Again, he hesitates. But he at least seems aware of how much his hesitation is bugging me now. Another couple of seconds, and he puts me out of my misery.

'Or the things we could all do together.'

'And is that so bad either?' I say, because really, what else am I supposed to go with? I'm practically drooling as it is. Anything less than approval would look like I'm just pulling nonsense out of my ass.

'I don't know. Do you think we're assholes?'

Lord, he looks so *sad* as he says it. As though that's a real possibility!

'I never thought you were assholes,' I tell him, in this kindly sort of voice that in no way fits how I'm really feeling. Mostly, I just want to scream from the rooftops: *You liked me so much that you had graphic chats about my backside. Halle-fucking-lujah.*

But thankfully he kind of side-blinds me again, in a way that stops all embarrassing exclamations dead.

'So why did you run out on us?' he asks, after which I can barely think of one little quiet word to say, never mind a bunch of loudly blurted ones. Is that what it looked like to them – that I ran out on them? I mean, I sort of suspected, but even so.

That's a little grimmer than I want to really deal with.

'Because … because you're beautiful and golden and perfect,' I say, before I've even really considered if that's true. It seems stupid once it's out there, but I can't deny – it has a certain raw ring to it. 'I don't know … I was scared. Weren't you scared? You're scared now, even though I came on to you and I touched you and now I'm the one bringing all of this up.' I run out of breath around sentence two, and keep going on sheer willpower alone. Even I'm marvelling by the time I get to: 'Man, I can't believe I'm bringing all of this up.'

But it sets him at ease, at least. His shoulders go down and those hands stop wringing each other. Then, after a moment of silence that's not quite comfortable, he cracks a faint smile. He puts his wriggling fingers over mine. 'I'm glad you did. I feel less weird about it now.'

I wonder just how long he has been feeling weird about it, though of course I don't say. I'm too busy mulling all of this over and over in my head, until I get to the one thing that sticks out a mile. 'Do you think Tyler's gay?'

He goes very still, but it doesn't seem to be out of shock. 'What – you mean like he's using my intense burning desire for you to get at me?'

'Exactly like that,' I say, and nod, just for good measure. I'm sure and certain in my weird theories on stuff I know nothing about. Until he throws me again.

'I think Tyler would fuck a hole in the wall if there

was nothing else available. That's what I think about Tyler.'

I can't help it – I blurt out a laugh. But in my defence, he started it.

'But don't you ... I don't know. Don't you ever feel like he took advantage of you?'

What can I say? It looks that way to me. Brandon had a little crush and Tyler had a lot of charm at his disposal, and he just talked his friend right into being a horny fucker. Sounds like a good all-round plan, if you ask me.

Even if Brandon doesn't think so. 'It's not like that. It's not like he ever makes me do stuff.'

I note that he said 'makes', present tense, but let it slide. 'It's kind of exactly like that.'

'No. No, it's not. It's the illusion of being made to do something. He talks like that and I feel all worked up and like I have no choice but to act, but it's not that. I have a choice. I can just ... pretend that I don't. I sit there and listen to him going on about you and how you'd look and feel and taste, and then when you come back from the kitchen I'm so horny that it's easy.'

And now I note that he said 'kitchen' in a very specific sort of way.

'Is that what actually happened?'

He takes a breath and half rolls his eyes, but I can see how nervous the question has made him. His shoulders have tightened again, just a little. And it's obvious he's resisting that hand twisting.

'Of course that's what actually happened. What? You haven't really thought all this time that I just spontaneously decided to lift your top up, have you? Come on.'

He's got a point. At the time I hadn't really thought about it – I hadn't really thought about anything, in truth. But now that I step back and consider it, I can see what he means. Brandon was always the one to hang back, to ask nervous questions, to say *don't, don't*. He would never have done that sort of stuff without a little cajoling.

And now I can see just who the cajoler was in that scenario.

It's the guy who walks through the front door a second later, grocery bags in the loop of his big arm. A look on his face like the one he always has – Y*eah, I know what you've been talking about. I know what you want, and what you need, and what's going to happen now. The only question is, what do you want to do about it?*

Chapter Five

The coffee he brings back is just what I need: strong, thick and barely tasting like coffee at all. I've no clue where he got it from but that sucker has so much sugar in it – so much syrup and foam and extra other stuff – that after I've finished it I feel like I've just been attached to the nearest electrical outlet.

Things get brighter. Clearer. Safer. We even watch a little morning television together, as though we've suddenly become the strangest married unit in all of existence. There's even some breakfast to go with it – from yet another heavenly place that can't possibly be real – and then a nice hot shower.

Everything is almost totally normal. Apart from the face palming I keep doing each time I go over sections of the conversation I just had. And how naked I feel when I walk out of the bathroom, in just some too big boxer shorts and a humongous T-shirt of Tyler's. Seriously, this thing hits my knees, and I still find myself squirming around inside of it.

They're going to see my bare legs. And my bare feet. And probably a bunch of other stuff that I don't want to think about too hard, as I retake my seat at the make-shift dining room table, in a dining room that doesn't actually exist. It's all just one big L-shaped room, really, with a kitchen and a bathroom tucked into the side of it – though I can see how it could be nice. It's really quite a big place, all open-plan. Sunlight coming in from those immense windows, bare boards just waiting for a bit of sanding and some wax.

The five years of repression and hidden feelings are probably just making the room seem smaller.

'That nice?' Tyler says, as innocent as a new lamb in spring. It's really not his fault that I read the words differently, and end up thinking about the conversation I've just had. Or maybe the night before, when he'd said very similar words about something else altogether.

'The shower? Yeah, it was great.'

Here would be a perfect time to tell them I need to get going. All I have to do is mention something more plausible than dry cleaning: a dog I need to take care of, or some work-related business that requires my attention.

Even though I'm a librarian and I don't have a dog, and most of all:

I don't want to. I don't want to.

I just want to hold my breath, and wait to see what Tyler says next.

'So did you tell Bran you overheard? Or is this the first anyone's hearing about it?'

OK, I did not expect *that* to be the thing he said next. I honestly didn't. At the very least I thought he was going to sort of … ease us into further discussion. Maybe ask a question or two about what we'd talked over, in his absence, or offer me some more of those amazing bagels.

Not this. This puts both me and Bran on edge immediately.

'We talked about … some stuff,' I say, carefully. Then, when the ground in front of me seems safe, I carry on. 'Bran mentioned that you guys … uh … used to talk about me. Sometimes.'

The corner of Tyler's mouth twitches, but he doesn't smile. No, he just let's all of his amusement show in those sultry eyes of his, as he leans back in a chair that's far too small for him. He almost looks like a giant who found this furniture down the beanstalk, and the clothes he's wearing don't help: a V-necked T-shirt that somehow shows a huge amount of chest hair, the material stretched taut over his solid chest; sweatpants that look suspiciously like the ones Brandon is wearing, only on Tyler they're low and tight around the ass and kind of obscene, if I'm being really honest.

Did he go out like that? And, if so, did a lot of people stare at the thick outline of his cock – the one that can be clearly seen along the length of his thigh? Because, God knows, I would stare, if I was out and about and that thing was coming towards me.

'Did he really? Well. I'm almost proud,' he says, and I think Brandon gets close to punching him. Only that voice saves his hide – syrup-thick and absolutely delicious. It turns Brandon's face red, even as he spreads his hands over the table and tries to keep things calm.

'I just explained to Maisie that we weren't trying to be assholes. That we liked her, and occasionally had … conversations about … about –'

'Doing her?'

'Ty!' Brandon protests, and when he does he slaps a hand down on the table, too – just for emphasis. No means no, and all that. You're crossing a line, stop.

But Tyler doesn't stop. Far from it, in fact. 'Though the word "doing" doesn't really encompass everything, don't you think? I mean, we talked about licking her ass and having her blow us both at the same time … what was your favourite, again? Oh yeah. The shower.'

'Don't tell her about the shower,' Brandon says, his glare so intense I'm only surprised it doesn't set Tyler on fire. And if his eyes don't do it then his voice sure should, because his voice has dropped so low I'm expecting an exorcist to show up at any moment.

But again, Tyler doesn't seem to care in the slightest. 'So, basically, we'd be in those communal showers outside the college pool – you know the ones?'

I nod as though I'm on strings.

'And maybe … I don't know, things get a little heated.'

Oh my God, oh my God. He's saying what I think he's saying, right? And if he's not saying that, then why is Brandon having some sort of respiratory attack right across from me?

'Could just be something fairly innocent, like a bit of soapy jerking off. Could be something a little more than that.'

'Don't tell her about more than that,' Brandon warns, but Tyler's on a roll, now.

'What? Like I get down on my knees and suck your cock? Because I seem to recall you liking that part of this little fantasy. Gives it an edge, don't you think? Something more than *just some guys having a circle jerk*. And besides, if I'm on my knees sucking you off, or you're on your knees sucking me off, it gives Maisie something to be really shocked about when she walks in on us both.'

His logic is impeccable, I have to say. I mean, if they were just jerking off they could probably hide it, before I saw anything. But you can't hide being on your knees with a cock in your mouth, you just can't. My mind can't even hide from the technicolour image of it happening, even though it never actually did.

'I think she's really shocked *now*. And probably about to run off on us.'

'You sure about that? Maybe you should ask her. Or better yet, actually see the signs of someone being aroused, rather than going around with your blinders on.'

The second he's said it I have the overwhelming urge to cover my nipples. And my pink cheeks. And maybe my groin while I'm at it, because by this point it must be glowing like a neon sign: ENTER HERE.

But I think it's best that I don't. I'd far rather have Brandon looking at me and knowing that I'm cool with all of this, instead of seeing him fret and fumble over it. He's almost as red as I feel, and every time Tyler says some incendiary thing his hands go to his hair – like last night, only worse.

It has to be worse. Now we're talking about man-on-man action in some communal showers, like a gay porn version of the life he probably thinks he's leading.

'You know, he's right – I'm really not bothered. Even if you were both a little … gay … I wouldn't mind.'

Brandon's hand slides down over his eyes, but Tyler seems completely unfazed.

As usual.

'I think *a little gay* is usually called *being bisexual*.

But I can see where you'd be confused. Being bisexual is like being the tooth fairy – very few people actually believe in you.'

'Do I have to clap my hands so you don't die?' I say, and am really proud of myself for doing so. Most of my body wants to collapse in on itself like a dying star, so really it's a miracle I'm managing to talk at all.

'I think you might have to clap your hands so Bran doesn't die,' he replies, because he's so smooth and sharp and also really, really right. I glance across at Brandon, only to find he's slid so far down in his chair he's almost underneath the table again – not to mention the fingers he's split over his eyes.

This is a horror movie, apparently, and he can't bear to watch too closely.

'Bran said that you'd fuck a hole in the wall if it was the least bit accommodating,' I say, like some tattletale out of school. I don't even know why, really. It just bursts out of me, along with most of my dignity and a soupçon of that neon arousal.

'I didn't say it like that,' Brandon protests, and in all fairness to him he's right. It's important that we keep the record straight.

'No. He said it more like you're just really horny.'

'That's probably true. But he's being a little disingenuous there – he's just as wildly horny as I am. In fact, I'd say he's so horny I could get him to do just about anything simply by talking about your tits for a while,' Tyler says, and after he's done I realise that I'm hanging halfway across the table. I'm almost out of my chair, like some gawker at the scene of an accident.

'So, I guess you're both just … two big, horny, gorgeous guys. Who like my breasts,' I manage to push out, but it takes some effort. I'm short of breath by the time I'm done.

'I guess we are. You want to do something about that?'

Oh God. Oh God.

'About what?'

'About our horniness.' Tyler pauses – probably to give the whole thing a little more weight. A little more tension. 'Unless you think we should do something about you first.'

I almost say it: *What needs doing with me?* And only catch myself at the very last, crucial second. Another moment and I'd have been all the way over, into crazy porn land.

Despite the fact that we're already *in* crazy porn land.

'Bet you're so wet right now, huh? All night with nowhere to go. Bet you're half crazy,' he says, and I can't tell him what I want to – that he's absolutely correct, of course he is. I have to just sit there, while my heart pounds in all the parts I usually use for speech.

'Come here, baby,' Tyler says, but he doesn't stop there. Once I've been hypnotised into standing up, he barrels straight into further, lewder instruction. 'Lift that T-shirt.'

And though I can hear Brandon somewhere in the background, telling me that I don't have to if I don't want to, I'm not really paying attention. The magician has spoken his spell, and I'm compelled to obey.

'Now take those cute little shorts down,' he says, and I obey that, too. I have to. His foggy gaze is like a hypnotist's trick and, after a moment of it, I can't resist. I wriggle the cottony material down my legs and off, so that when I straighten back up again he can see every-thing – my smoothly waxed mons, my pouting pussy lips. Even with my legs mostly closed, I'm pretty sure he can make out the protruding tip of my stiff clit.

I must look obscene, and not just because of those two things.

'Ohhhh yeah. Look how wet you are, baby,' he purrs, then turns to an almost crazed Brandon. 'I told you she'd be this wet. Look at it all over her legs and her sweet little mound. Come on, baby, come here.'

He doesn't wait for me to comply this time, however. He just leans forwards and gets me around the waist, then reels me in as though it's nothing. It's not a big deal that I'm naked, and it's not a big deal that he lifts me off my feet a moment later before spreading me out over the table.

But it is a big deal that the word 'spread' is in there.

The second I've got my back to the wood he shoves my thighs apart and, when I gasp and maybe struggle a little, he holds me there. He keeps me like this, cunt completely exposed and open. Everything is on view for both of them, in a way I've never experienced before.

I'm not even sure if I've ever had one man looking at me like this, never mind two. And he doesn't stop with the hands splayed on my thighs, and that hypnotist's gaze on my exposed sex. He uses two fingers to stroke through all the mess I've made, until everything is there for him to see and talk about.

'Ohhh you're soaking. How long have you been this way, huh? How long did you listen to us talking, with your clit all swollen like this?'

On the word 'clit' he just feathers over the tip of it, but embarrassingly, it's almost enough to put me over the edge. Pleasure clenches right around that spot and then kicks outwards, leaving me gasping and moaning. I think I even say one or both of their names.

Shortly before Tyler has mercy on me, and bends to lick where his fingers have just been.

Somewhere to the right of me, Bran chokes out a 'holy crap', but I don't mind. I understand. I want to use the exact same words myself the second Tyler starts rubbing and working that slippery tongue over my aching bud. It's just too much all at once, too intense, and I try to get away at the feel of it. I buck my hips, and squirm.

But that just gives him the opportunity to slide two fingers into me, so sudden and shocking and most of all – *easy*. There's no sense of pressure or hint of burn. I'm so slippery he just fucks right into me, slow at first, but then with a little more intent. Soon it's three fingers instead of two, and then he's hitting that bundle of nerves inside me, over and over, while his tongue makes those tight, slick circles around my clit.

It's unbearable. I want to clamp my legs together, but of course I can't. I'm trapped by his broad hands, digging into my thighs, and by a sensation so intense it's almost like burning. He flicks over the underside of my swollen bud in this maddening, awful way, and there's nothing I can do to stop it. I can't even tell him not to, because all that comes out when I try is, 'Uhhhh, yeah, you're gonna make me come.'

I don't think I've ever said anything like that to another living soul, but it's impossible to deny. Thirty seconds in and I'm totally going to do it, because of the thick thrust of his fingers and the greedy feel of his tongue. Even the sounds he's making get me closer – all these breathy, hot groans that gust over my overheated flesh.

And then Brandon joins him in song and, oh, I don't know what to do.

'Yeah, go on, do it to her,' he says, as though he's become a different person. It's just like before, only this time I get to see exactly how he looks when it happens.

74

His face is flushed and his eyes are glazed, and they don't fix on me with the usual mixture of patience and concern. Instead, they slide over my body, taking in all the sights as they go.

And as for Bran's mouth ... oh God, his mouth. Tyler was right – he is just magnificently horny. I've never seen anyone look so ready to fuck in all my days. His tongue is poking up into the corner of his upper lip, like there really is some erogenous zone there that I don't know about.

And he's ... he's doing other stuff, too. He's got a hand over his right pec, but it's not just lingering there. Once I manage to focus I can actually see: he's pinching his own nipple, between thumb and forefinger. He's plucking at it, in a way I've never seen any other man do.

And of course he's hard. He's so hard his cock has made a little wet spot on the loose material of his sweatpants. Another second and he'll be masturbating, I know it, and I don't mind admitting that I want to hold off for that. I do, oh I do.

But I can't. Tyler gives one last lick over the underside of my clit and my orgasm grabs a hold of me, too tight to bear. I almost scream against my gritted teeth, and I know I go rigid. There's just nothing I can do about it. The pleasure drums through me, jerking my helpless body as it goes.

And then once it's done there's just this relief. Intense,

beautiful relief, as though all of these years have actually been an endurance test of some kind and finally, finally I've made it over the finishing line. I broke the tape, and now I'm a limp rag by the drinks stand, gulping down oxygen and victory, in equal measures.

Though as I lie there, basking, I neglect one vital component in said victory. I mean, *I* might be satisfied, but the guy who got me to that satisfied place certainly isn't. I'm not even sure if ten per cent of Tyler's kinky desires have been used up, in all honesty, because after a moment of limp bliss I hear him say to Brandon, loud and clear, 'Here. Taste her. Taste her.'

Of course, I have to look. What sort of fool wouldn't? My good and very hunky friend Tyler is offering his glistening fingers to my good and very hunky friend Brandon, and when I turn my head I'm just in time to see that neat, square mouth devouring what he's been offered – with *gusto*.

I don't think I've ever seen Brandon do anything with gusto. And it's a real sight to see, too – those eyes of his half closed and almost mean seeming, mouth working and working around those two fingers, as though it's nothing at all.

Yeah, we can just do this now. We suck and fuck each other and get totally lost in pleasure, even if the pleasure makes us insane. Which I think it has, because a moment later Tyler one-ups this dirty little show they're putting on.

He waits, I think, until Brandon is in that state of dazed complicity. And then he slides his sweatpants down one-handed, and says the words that will probably haunt my masturbation fantasies for the next one thousand years: 'You want to suck something else?'

Oh God, something *else*. And he's clearly not talking about his big toe. You couldn't possibly mistake what he's saying, because the thing he's just revealed isn't exactly overlook-able. It's bigger than I remember, and thicker, and it juts out from the nest of oddly dark hair at his groin like an accusation. Like a *command*.

Do it.

And Brandon *does*.

He doesn't hesitate, or shoot a surreptitious glance at me. He just pours off his chair and onto the floor, then takes that heavy, swollen prick into his mouth – so greedy for it he doesn't even stop to catch his breath. It's almost embarrassing for me to watch, because I know I've never gotten up this level of sloppy enthusiasm. He sucks so hard and so wetly I almost wish I had a cock so I might know how incredible this must feel.

Though Tyler does, at least, give me some approximation. 'Yeah, make it nice and wet. Do it just like that – suck me off, you little cocksucker.'

And he also says some other things, too. Things I do not know how to process – I mean, does Brandon enjoy being talked to in such a brutish, mean sort of manner?

77

Somehow I can't imagine he does ... until I realise he's actually jerking off, as he swallows Tyler's cock.

He's got his hand inside his pants, but even that's not enough. After a second of frantic rubbing, he pulls his cock free and jerks at his own stiff length as he laps and sucks at Tyler's. I swear, all I can hear are the thick, slick sounds of fucking, and all I can see are hard cocks being pleasured, and then Tyler says, 'You want some, Maisie?'

And I float up, out of my body, to watch all of this from someplace safe. I have the overwhelming urge to check over my shoulder, just in case there's another hotter, dirtier girl lying on the table behind me.

I know there isn't. There's just me, and Tyler, and Brandon, and Tyler is fucking Brandon's face with his meaty cock, and Brandon is moaning and sucking and stroking himself, so really, who's the odd man out, here? I'd practically be a social pariah, if I didn't at least nod my head. And maybe fumble my way off this table, until I'm somehow on my knees, too.

I've got a close-up, then, of Tyler's cock easing in and out of Brandon's mouth. All that slick spit greasing the way. The flicker of his tongue over the flared head, just before the whole thing sinks back in. It's delicious, unbearable – and yet when Tyler forces his friend back and exposes all of that thick length, something clenches low down in my belly.

I think it's nerves. Or arousal. Or a mixture of the

two. And it comes again – harder – when Tyler offers his dick to me. I'm going to taste Brandon on him, I think, deliriously, but the idea doesn't stop me. I want to do this dirty thing, even though Brandon echoes some of my concerns a second later.

'You don't have to be a part of this,' he says, but that's both the problem and the allure of it. Being a part of something – something sexy and forbidden and full of delicious promise.

A little piece of me wants to say no and end it. But most of me wants to say yes.

Yes, I think, and then I lean forwards and part my lips around the sweet swell of his cock. Slow, at first, but, oh, when he groans for me, when he gives me a sound that has as much abandon as Brandon usually does, I can't stop myself descending into frantic. I suck hard, licking and licking to get more of that taste – different to Brandon's salt-sweet cock, but with a hint of his mouth at the back of it – greedy for it before I'm even sure I want to be.

Though I'm surer after he speaks.

'You want it? Huh? I'm gonna do it in your mouth.'

Yeah, I'm sure then. I glance up at him and he's near shaking, face as flushed as Brandon's, nipples making tight little points through his shirt. It's arresting to see him like that but even more so to feel him this out of control, and I push for a bit extra.

I want him to fuck my mouth, I realise. I want him to be rough with me the way he was with Brandon, but he holds back. Just a little. Just enough for it to surprise me when his head goes back and his hips jerk forwards, and his thick, creamy spend floods my mouth.

'Ohhh yeah,' he tells me. 'Keep going, keep going, I'm coming.'

But he really doesn't have to explain. Even if he wasn't spurting all over my tongue, I can actually feel his cock swelling and jerking. He's trembling, too – little spasms that make me crazy and remind me of how it felt for me to climax so viciously and hardly be able to think through any of it.

I can hardly think now. I drown in the sounds of both my men going over, first in the guttural but reined-in groans that Tyler gives me, and then the much bolder, brighter cries of pleasure from Brandon, as he gives me what I never thought he could. He stands up for his orgasm and instead of tamely splashing my belly or my breasts he coats the place Tyler's just finished filling.

He covers my lips and my chin and my cheek with his come, until I'm nothing but a used up mess. I'm a cock-sucking slut, too, but that's not half the insult it used to be in my head.

It's like a badge of honour, instead.

Chapter Six

I don't know what to do, once it's done – and that's probably how I end up taking another shower like a maniac. I stand under the hot spray and have ten imaginary conversations in my head, most of which start with the words *So what do we do now?* And finish with me returning to my monotonous life.

I'm not brave enough for this, I think. I'm the kind of person who started out at college dreaming of being a writer, and gradually eroded that dream down to a journalist, and then a teacher, and finally ended it with what I am: a librarian.

I can sense that I'm going to erode this, too. After all, I did that very thing last time. I took something sexy and risky and great and turned it into something I never wanted to think about ever again.

And now it's back, with reinforcements.

'Maisie?' Brandon calls through the bathroom door and, for this huge moment, I can't actually answer him. The words make this clicking sound in my throat, as my head floods with the images of all the things we just did. I just *did* them, like it didn't even matter. 'You OK in there? I'm just gonna put some clothes on the wash basket, OK?'

No, not OK, I think. You'll come in and see me naked!

But of course that's crazy. He just saw me naked about half an hour ago. He saw how pink and tight my nipples get when I'm excited, and how swollen and messy my pussy was. If he strains hard enough, he could probably recall it all from last time, too.

I don't know why I'm suddenly shy. When he comes in, I find myself moving to the back of the rickety shower, so that he won't see me through the frosted door. And, once he's left the clothes, I dart out like a criminal, drying hastily and shoving all the stupid things on, before anyone can catch me.

I feel like a fool, afterwards – and not just because of my still-wet skin and my misplaced embarrassment. There's also the fact that I'm wearing an old college jersey of Tyler's, and a pair of jeans of Brandon's, and both things are so immense on me I can hardly walk. The hems trail off my feet like flippers. I have to roll up the sleeves, just to make sure I still have hands.

And naturally they both laugh when they see me – Brandon in an apologetic sort of way, Tyler … less so.

'I don't understand why you didn't bring anything with you,' he says, as though it's that simple for him, to pack a bag full of assumptions and bust down the door of a life you stopped leading years ago.

He should know that it isn't. I'm struggling just to keep myself here, in front of the bed they've both sprawled themselves across. Tyler isn't even wearing a shirt – he's just got that pair of sweatpants on, and even that item of clothing doesn't scream innocence. All I can see behind my eyes is how he looked when he pulled them down one-handed. That move he made … so desperate, and yet so not at the same time.

It's like he's somehow above his own desires, looking down on them. And they can take hold of him and do things to him, and even make him a little crazy, but they can't take away his awareness of what's happening. He can't be hypnotised, the way we can.

'I … um … I just …' I say, in the absence of the things I really want to mention. Thankfully, however, Brandon saves me.

'You OK?' he says, then even sweeter: 'Sorry about the clothes. Didn't want to give you your old ones, but ours are obviously much bigger than I'd expected them to be on you.'

That's the understatement of the year. I have to actually hold the jeans up in one bunched fist, and those hem-flippers aren't getting any easier to move around in. Plus, that awareness of how naked I am inside the clothes … it's getting almost vicious, now. When I yank the jeans up the seam slips between the still tender lips of my pussy, and rubs right over my clit.

Which sounds like it hurts, I know.

But it doesn't.

'No, no it's fine. This is great,' I tell them both, which is true. It's not a big deal that I'm swamped in clothes – the opposite, in fact. The material protects me when Tyler lifts an arm as though to say, *Come on, come onto the bed and we'll snuggle*, and I crawl between them like a bomb expert, determined not to detonate anything. Something's bound to go off, any second – I know it.

Only it doesn't.

We all just lie there and watch a movie together, while my body hums and hums crazily. Brandon holds my hand and Tyler strokes my hair. Sometimes they shift around and sprawl across me, just like they used to.

But nothing else. They don't try anything, or say anything, to the point where I start thinking I imagined it all – though of course I know I didn't.

* * *

These peaks keep really happening, these swells, and, after they've receded, I'm left stranded on a beach of TV watching and Chinese take-outs and short trips into town. There are cakes in cute cafés and viewing of sights, as though I am on vacation and Brandon and Tyler are my tour guides. They show me where I can buy clothes, and we take pictures together in a photo booth. In all four I look bright, happy, relaxed.

So why am I tense inside? Why am I in a state of incredible waiting? I keep feeling these words on the end of my tongue: *If you want to again, we can. It can be that kind of vacation, you know?*

But somehow I always stop short, as though the carousel has gone around and it's not my turn any more. Tyler has to say, I think. I see him stood by the railings around the river, looking out over the city as it fades into dusk. And he just looks so ... dark. So commanding. Command us, I think at him.

But he doesn't. And on the third day of this happy vacation, I realise: he's not waiting to make his next move, he's waiting for me to make mine.

* * *

It's the kind of restaurant I've never actually been to. The seats are expensive to the point of uncomfortable and the waiter barely speaks. He just gestures impeccably and Tyler seems to interpret his code, and then we all have glasses of wine I can't drink.

It tastes like the insides of someone's musty shoe, but I fail to say anything. Tyler's just made a toast about old friends reuniting, and there was a touch of poetry in there. I'd be the odd man out again if I behaved as awkwardly as I feel.

Even Brandon looks like he's been carved out of classiness. He's wearing a suit – this one definitely picked out by Tyler, because apparently Tyler is some sort of clothes-obsessed fashion guru and this time I saw him do it – and his hair has been done just so. It lies in a thick, handsome swatch across his forehead and seems to make him look just a touch older. A touch more weathered.

I flounder in a glittering confection I didn't want to wear, the neckline of which is digging into my bust. Even the mute waiter has something to say about my cleavage, when he oozes back to the table. I see him glance at everything that's overflowing, as though I'm some cheap floozy.

Oh, how I wish I were just some cheap floozy, instead of the skittish thing I am. All we've talked about for days is, in no particular order: our favourite '80s cartoons, what we'd like to order for dinner and past relationships we've had that didn't really work out. Brandon disliked a girlfriend of Tyler's called Cynthia. Cynthia wanted Tyler to buy her a BMW, apparently. And Brandon once had a serious relationship with a girl called Tiffany, but now thinks it's as hilarious as we do that he could ever think someone called Tiffany could be serious about anything.

And then there was me. I didn't say anything, because my motley crew of misfits and rejects can't really compete with someone who wanted Tyler for his trust fund, and a girl who once told Brandon that eating solid foods is bad for you.

And I can't say much now, either, because apparently we're talking about real-estate investments. Lord, I just don't know what to do. How do I interrupt all of this ... stylishness? What's the best way to introduce a topic of this nature, with the optimum of elegance and wit?

'Guys, you do remember we had a threesome the other day, right?'

Somehow, I don't think I've quite hit the mark I was aiming for. Tyler actually raises an eyebrow at me and Brandon chokes on his wine. Both expressions of surprise are about equal, I think, when you consider the people who are making them.

'I vaguely recall,' Tyler says, as he lounges back against his seat. It's impossible to do so, however. I don't how he's managing it, because these seats are like iron.

'And you don't think we should have a chat about that? I mean, wasn't that the problem last time?'

'I thought the problem was that you disappeared for five years,' Tyler says. 'But do go on.'

I think it's pretty clear that I don't want to, after words like those. Though it's not because they hurt me a little – which they do – or that Brandon kind of gasps, once they're said. It's more for the surprise of it.

I didn't think he cared that much.

Brandon, yes. Tyler, no.

'You know I'm sorry about that, right?' I ask, but he shocks me again.

'No, no, you misunderstand me. I'm not angry that you ran away. I'm concerned that you're going to do it again.'

Brandon holds up a hand, at that – which is fortunate. I'm too dazed to do anything but stare at Tyler and his sudden ability to have emotions.

'What Tyler means is ...' Brandon starts, but he doesn't have to explain. I get the picture, loud and clear: Tyler feels the same way Brandon does. He feels abandoned too. I can see it all over his face, before Brandon goes any further. 'We just don't want to scare you away again. Or make you think that this is all some ... weird game.'

Tyler nods at that, but it's his expression that's the peach. It slides all the way back up from tense to amused acceptance. And then he illustrates the reason for this amused acceptance, just for me.

'It's my fault that it comes across as a weird game. I just enjoy them so,' he says, in this smooth, slick way that somehow arouses me as much as it warms my heart. He wants me to be reassured, I think. He wants me to want all of this, and to know that he wants it too, but above all of that is the idea that I be as comfortable as humanly possible, while discussing threesomes.

And I think … I think I love him a little bit for that. I think I love them both for being so careful and considerate, and for saying things like: 'We just wanted to make sure you knew that we want to talk *with* you. Not just about … your vagina, behind your back.'

I fight the urge to burst out laughing. Of course, it's all really clear then: the tea and cakes, the faux-vacation, the sense of unbearable tension trying to crush my soul all the time. And then there are the conversations we've been having …

'Is that why we've been having so many chats about '80s cartoons?' I ask, in a sudden rush of understanding. Thankfully, Brandon has the decency to look sheepish.

'We were trying to show you that we don't see you as a …' Brandon starts.

'A sex object,' Tyler finishes.

I almost laugh again, only this time it feels even less appropriate. They both seem scarily serious about this, in a way I hadn't fully processed the last time Brandon said. He'd told me about his worries, that I might see him as an asshole. But I don't think I'd appreciated how deep that went.

'Guys, I really don't think it's a big deal that you talk about me or … or fantasise about me. It's actually a relief, in a way, because ... well, I do it about you. I mean, isn't that how it's supposed to be? You fancy someone and they fancy you and then you kind of think about doing stuff with them?'

They glance at each other and, for one awful moment, I'm sure I've said the wrong thing. I haven't taken into account the fact that this isn't just boy meets girl, and in bypassing that I've exposed myself as a heinous pervert, who doesn't mind threesomes. Who will, in fact, accept them, as long as she knows that the two guys involved totally dig her and aren't just fucking around.

But then Tyler eyes me quizzically, and says, 'You fantasise about us?'

And I realise I've made a critical error. 'Well, I ...'

'As in, you think about us doing stuff to you, while you ... you know,' Brandon says, and he does it in the nicest way possible, he really does. He uses a vague term instead of the actual word 'masturbate', and he doesn't make any sort of illustrative gestures with his hands. I'm not suddenly forced to imagine a giant clitoris, hovering in the air in front of him.

It's just that I'm starting to feel trapped, regardless. I seem to be clenching at the leather I'm sitting on, and my shoulders have gone all tense, and I can feel my heart fluttering in my chest. I'm not even sure why, but it's there – and it gets worse the longer this staring contest goes on. They're waiting for an answer, I know.

But this is the only one I have to give: 'Why is *this* the weird thing? You guys … you guys jerked off together while talking about fucking me!'

'True,' Tyler says, as he does something cool and deliberate like finger the stem of his wine glass. 'But we didn't know you liked that idea.'

'I didn't say I did,' I tell him, then immediately regret it. The words just make Brandon even more skittish than he is already, like I've accused him of something or exposed *him* as the pervert.

Though if that is what I'm doing, it's only to take the heat off myself. I'm a coward, and a fool – one who can't even answer simple questions, like this one: 'Then tell us what you do like.'

A million images buzz through my mind, but instead of illustrating any of them, I find myself turning to look at the restaurant patrons just over my shoulder. There's a woman not ten feet from us, wearing a dress made out of sheerest class. In fact, everyone in here is dressed in sheerest class. The whole place is dripping with elegance, from the tasteful lighting that ensures no one looks a day over twenty, to the alpine white of the snapped smooth tablecloths.

But Tyler doesn't seem to care. We could be anywhere, to him. We could be in a filthy alley, getting ready to make some sort of seedy exchange. *You can hear what I have to say, if you give me the stuff first.*

Though of course the stuff, in this instance, is Tyler's hand in Brandon's lap.

Good Lord, he absolutely has a hand in Brandon's lap.

'I don't know.'

'You do know. Tell us. We've told you. Now you tell us.'

It seems only fair, when he puts it like that.

'Well, you know. Just ordinary things, really. I used to imagine that instead of studying, we'd … kiss.'

'How scandalous,' Tyler says, then for extra emphasis he does something to Brandon that makes Brandon very unhappy. Or absolutely ecstatic, depending on your point of view. His face turns pink and his mouth comes open, which looks like a good thing. But he also turns his head away from the main hub of the restaurant, and jerks a hand down over Tyler's – like an appeal to stop.

I think. I think.

'And was there anything else, aside from kissing?'

'I can't say it here.'

'Why not? I'm stroking Bran's cock here. In fact, I've done it before. He loves a bit of public exhibitionism. Don't *you*, Maisie? Don't you like seeing him try to pretend that he's not getting off right now? And all of these people, too … all of them so smooth and suave and pristine. What would they think, if they knew you were wet over watching me masturbate another man?'

For the first time in my life I wish I enjoyed the taste of wine. I could really do with drinking a whole glass of the stuff, right now – down in one. Or maybe I could get away with signalling a waiter, and ordering something stiffer.

Like battery acid.

'Maybe we should go. I think you're making him uncomfortable,' I say, though that's still only partially true. Brandon's now studying the wall by Tyler's head with a kind of furtive, jerky intensity, but at the same time, I can tell how much he's enjoying this. His teeth are deep in his lower lip, and that hand he's got over Tyler's …

I don't think he's restraining it, exactly.

'I tell you what, Maisie. We can go, when you give me a fantasy. Just one fantasy you used to have about us,' Tyler says.

I rack my brains, I really do. But mostly what I come up with is: *We all sit in a restaurant while you masturbate Brandon under the table. And eventually maybe my eyes fall out of my head.*

'Come on,' he says, only this time I don't struggle half as much. Instead my head floods with memories of things that didn't actually happen, like the fuck they never gave me, right after they'd finished covering me with their come. Brandon and then Tyler? I wonder. Or both at the same time?

And then I just blurt it out. 'OK. OK. Sometimes I used to imagine you ... one of you having sex with me. And maybe the other ...*you know*.'

Tyler's eyes narrow to slits for those last two words, and I know what's coming next. My doom, that's what. I'm done for here.

'I'm afraid we don't know, do we, Brandon?' he says and, as he does so, his arm jerks in a very particular sort of way – one that makes Brandon have to stifle a moan, into his fist. 'Maybe you should explain a little more fully.'

I grit my teeth, but manage to get something out. 'You understand what I'm saying,' I tell him, but he gives me nothing, absolutely nothing. No quarter now. It's too late for holding back and being coy.

'I don't. You're really going to have to be more graphic.'

I get a little flash of him teasing me, with that thick cock of his – rubbing it over my cheek and my lips, until I open up for him.

'I suck your cock,' I say, under my breath. But under my breath isn't good enough for Tyler. The words on their own aren't enough for Tyler. He wants more, before I'm even willing to give it.

'You can do better than that, Maisie,' he says, and the thing is, he's right. My cheeks are scorching hot and I can practically feel the pressure of a million classy eyes on me, but the graphic version is there, inside me. I can be like Tyler if I really force myself.

'I let you fuck my face,' I tell him, and after that it's a little easier. Like pulling the cork out and watching the liquid spill free. 'You fuck my face while he fills my cunt.'

'I see,' he says, which sounds just as deliberate and in control as he was before. But there's something in his expression, now – a tension – and his eyes are fogged over. He liked that one, I think.

And he likes the next one even more.

'And while you're thrusting your big cock down my throat, you tell him how to do it. Hard, really hard, until I really want to scream – though of course I can't.'

'Why can't you?' he asks, and I know I've got him now. He'd never go with such a stupid question, if he had a complete hold on all of his senses. I think he even knows he's lost it once he's said it, because he tries to sit up a little straighter and look at something that isn't me.

But it's too late.

'Because you're so hot and swollen in my mouth. I can hardly do anything at all,' I say.

He nods, like that's perfectly understandable. He's a kindly therapist, teasing out all of my little kinks and foibles.

As he jerks off the guy next to him.

'I see. And you like that?' he asks, while Brandon

practically curls against his side. He's close, very close. I know this not because of the flush all over his face or his weird position, but because he isn't telling Brandon to stop squeezing this information out of me.

Quite the contrary. It seems to be driving him nuts.

'Yes.'

'You've thought about that.'

'Yes.'

'Tell me what else you've thought about,' Tyler says, and then somehow it's easy. We've got a rhythm going now, and it would be churlish of me to let it slide.

'You both taking turns. I used to ... I used to think about that a lot, while masturbating. I used to imagine one of you walking in while the other was fucking my pussy, and you'd say something like, "Come on over and try this."'

Brandon turns his head for that one, and settles his heated gaze on me – though it only makes me want to do more. Say more. A little bit more of this and he's going to come, I think, and not just because Tyler now has a hand inside his trousers, or is jerking him hard enough to make it obvious, all the way up through his arm. It's the things I'm saying.

'And then what?' Tyler asks, and I keep my eyes on Brandon as I answer.

'And then I'd let you. I'd lie there with my legs spread and watch you use me. Sometimes it would go further, in my head, depending on how long I'd been touching myself or how turned on I was.'

'How far?'

Yeah, how far? I think. How far do I have to go, until you come right here in this restaurant? And then Brandon chokes out a little sound, and I know it's not far at all.

'Occasionally, you didn't just fuck my pussy. One of you would say something rude, something awful, like "You wanna try her ass?" And then you'd fuck me there too,' I say. My face turns to molten lead, it really does. It's worth it, however, for the way it makes Brandon arch against Tyler and push into that working hand.

He's coming, I think, but that doesn't stop Tyler.

'One after the other?' he asks, as though he needs just a little something extra now, too. Not to come maybe, but certainly for his own gratification. And I know just what his gratification needs.

'Sometimes both at the same time,' I say. 'When I get close to coming, it doesn't seem to matter. I just want to suck and fuck, hard.'

He considers this, as calmly as someone might consider their dinner order. And then he sums it up, just in case I wasn't aware.

'So if we got you hot enough, you'd do just about anything,' he says, and I say yes, even though I know what that might mean. He could demand I get on the table right now, if he wanted to. He could make me spread my legs and take his cock, while everyone in here watched.

Only he doesn't.

He throws a fifty down instead, and points to the exit.

'Let's go,' he says, in a way that should leave me relieved.

It should. But I think I'd be a fool, if it did.

Chapter Seven

It's the most incredible sensation – two tongues swirling and slipping around my stiff clit, the feel of their hot, panted breaths against my spread sex, the sight of them, one dark, one light. I can hardly process all of it in one go, and have to keep taking short breathers. Eyes closed, and nothing but the physical sense of them licking my clit. Eyes open, and then I get to see it all. I get to see Tyler looking up at me from beneath hooded lids, as he near makes out with Brandon around my slippery folds.

Ten seconds of this and I'll come, I know it. It barely took me that to come last time, and that was just one man doing, while the other man watched. Now they're both sucking and licking me and, after a moment, more than sucking and licking me. I feel the firm press of someone's fingers at my greedy hole, followed by the slow, exquisite slide as one of them eases into me.

Though that's the thing, isn't it? It's one of them. It's some*one*. And I don't know what's more exciting – the sensation of a finger, working back and forth inside of me, or the idea that it could be either Brandon or Tyler.

Or both.

After a second of this, there's a sense of further pressure and then something else slips inside me. Another finger, as eager to explore as the first one. I'm getting fucked by both of them, I think, and then I remember what I said in the restaurant and blush right to the roots of my hair.

I did ask for them both, after all. I actually asked for both of their cocks inside me, and what's going on now is not exactly far from that. It's not even far in terms of size, because after a moment they're both working two fingers inside me, and I'm so slippery and open it hardly takes anything at all.

As Tyler is keen to point out. 'Look at that,' he says, in a way that should embarrass me. He pushes my thigh down flat against the bed, one-handed, and sits back a little – just to give them both a better view. And when Brandon sits back too I can see the look on his face. I can see how wet his mouth is, how heated his gaze is … I know how I must appear.

Like a slut, with her cunt spread to take all comers.

'You want to fuck her first?' Tyler says, then even worse: 'If you fuck her now, hard, she'll come on your cock. She's so ready she could come over just about anything.'

Oh, it's so humiliating. It's the most humiliating thing in the entire world … apart from the fact that he's right, of course. I'm so ready to climax I could clench my pussy around their fingers, and go off right this second. My clit's so swollen, so full of that sweet ache, a gust of air would be enough to push me over.

But he keeps me waiting just a little bit longer. They both do.

They take their time removing their suits, while I flounder on the bed. And once they're done with their suits they make sure I'm zipped out of my dress – though that sounds a little clinical for the way they actually go about. In reality, whenever something new is revealed – like my breasts, in this stupid, straining strapless bra – I am fondled and stroked, hands rubbing over my stiff nipples. Light slaps on my bare ass; fingers digging into various fleshy parts of my body.

By the time they're done I'm not a person any more. I'm just a body, waiting to be used. I'm just a trembling thing, ready and willing for the act I know they're going to get me to perform.

And it's the most aroused I've ever been in my entire life.

Tyler has to haul me into position. I can't do it myself. I've gone all limp and weird, and I keep trying to reach for him with something that isn't my hands – even though that's impossible. You can't reach for someone with your mouth. It's stupid to even try, and yet I'm doing it. I'm blindly feeling for him, for his cock, for just something, anything, and it means I'm not prepared when Brandon rubs the head of his condom-covered dick over my slippery entrance.

I jerk forwards almost immediately, but of course there's nowhere to go. There's a wall of Tyler in front of me, as heavy and solid as brick, and even if there wasn't, he has hands. He's capable of holding me steady, even if Brandon isn't.

'You sure you want –' he starts, but I think Tyler cuts him off. I feel his body move as though he's shaking his head, and then one big hand just slides down over my back. Like a soothing motion, I think, that's followed by the softest command I've ever heard.

'Pull her back to you,' he says and, after a moment of hesitation, I feel Brandon's hands around my thighs. He tugs, just a little, he prompts me and then he can see how willingly I go up onto all fours. Legs spread, back arched, ass in the air.

Go on, I think, go on, but he doesn't immediately. He waits, until I rub back against him. Until I'm half crazed and moaning, hands bunching too tightly in the sheets.

And then he just slides the head of his cock through my slippery folds, seeking entrance. Working and rubbing, slow and steady, until my cunt opens for that good, thick thing.

He's extremely hard. Or at least, he feels really hard, going in. I try to clench around the intrusion but there's no give there, no place for me to go, and once I've done it I hear him gasp. I feel him shudder, then hear Tyler's sardonic twang.

'Maybe you should take a second,' he says, but he's got no room to talk. The cock he's currently stroking right next to my face is so flushed, so slippery, I'm surprised he can manage to touch it at all. A few rough, slick jerks over the swollen head and he'll do it all over me, I know he will.

But I suspect he's not going to give in just yet.

'How does she feel?' he asks, but he doesn't stop at that level of tease. Apparently, he's not satisfied with watching me squirm, as he talks around me like I'm not there. He also has to stroke the tip of his cock over my parted lips, backing off when I try to lick or suck. Easing forwards when I keep myself perfectly still.

'Tight. Really tight. She keeps squeezing around me.'

'Yeah? She trying to milk that eager cock of yours?'

'Oh God, do you have to say stuff like that?' Brandon asks, and I understand how he feels. I'm almost beside myself now, and Tyler talking this way isn't helping.

'Like what? Like once, when we were jerking off

together, I just leaned down and licked the tip of your cock and you creamed all over my face?'

Yeah, it's not helping at all. The minute those words are out a great jolt of pleasure rolls through my body, and once it's done I can't help myself. I have to work myself back on Brandon's cock, just to keep myself sane.

I mean, did that really happen?

'Don't … don't …' Brandon says, which probably means it did. Back in college – back when I was innocently working on essays with them – they were sucking each other off and spurting all over each other's face and Lord only knows what else.

I might come if I think about what else.

'Are you going to cream in her tight little pussy? Tell me what it looks like first,' Tyler says, and I swear it almost happens then. I'm making a noise like some animal drowning, and I'm hanging on to one of his big legs as though it's a life raft. A couple more thrusts and I'll go over.

Unfortunate, really, that Tyler's words make Brandon slow, and then stop.

'What are you … do you …' he stutters, in a way that suggests he can no longer understand words. He's broken down, the way I have. I can barely do anything aside from rock back against his no longer moving cock, while blindly searching for Tyler's with my mouth.

And when he finally, finally slides that slick tip past my lips, it's a relief.

'Tell me what she looks like, spread around your cock,' Tyler says, while I do exactly what I told him I would. I suck at him, greedily, tongue lapping and swirling around the swollen head. He doesn't even have to put a hand in my hair, or thrust forwards.

I make myself gag on his thick length before he's done a single thing – and they both groan when I do. Like they like it, I think. They like hearing me force myself and take as much cock as I can, but more than that they like doing really dirty things to me, while talking about it in explicit detail.

'Uhhhh. Really wet. When I pull out, I can see it all glistening on me,' Brandon says, and, oh God, I can feel exactly what he means. I can feel his cock slowly easing out of me, everything so slippery and good.

Tyler starts to shake. It's the only outward sign he gives that this blow job is making him nuts – aside from the breathlessness of his voice, maybe. When he next speaks, he sounds like some whore I picked up, from that slave harem I thought of earlier.

'Yeah, that's good. More,' he says, and though he could be talking to me, here, I know he's not. He's waiting for Brandon to choke out something else, something lewder, as those glorious thrusts pick up again. Oh, he does it so hard – just like I wanted him to. And I can feel Tyler rocking his hips now, too, a little.

Like they're connected, through me.

'And she's all ... open ... ohhh God. Ohhh God, I'm gonna come,' Brandon groans, but I could have told him that. His cock swells in that tight, slick little passage, and those thrusts turn frantic. Another second, I think, another second ... but I don't have to say.

'Don't come yet. Not yet. She's close,' Tyler offers for me.

And he's right, despite Bran's next words.

'How can you tell?' he asks, and my face flushes red before Tyler even answers. I know what he's going to go with after all. I told them both, back at the restaurant – and I can no more help it than I can hold back the orgasm that's starting to swell through me.

'Cause she's sucking on me really hard ... Oh fuck, Maisie. Watch her. Watch her suck my cock. Look how greedy she is,' Tyler moans, while I die a little inside. I can hardly deny what he's saying after all. I'm working on his cock so frantically, so sloppily, that even I know how it must look.

Like I fucking love it.

'Ohhh yeah.'

'Fuck her hard, Bran. Fuck her hard, that's it,' Tyler says, and I'd be touched that he remembered, if I wasn't so mortified – not to mention absolutely stuffed full of surging pleasure. I can feel my body shuddering under the pressure, and I have to let go of Tyler. Just for a second.

Just long enough to groan ecstatically, at the thought of what's actually happening here. I'm coming. I'm coming, without a finger or mouth on my clit. Just Brandon, fucking into me hard enough to jolt me up the bed, while his filthy little mouth spews things I already know, but am more than glad to hear.

'Oh yeah, Maisie, yeah, do it on my cock. She's coming. Ohhhh, she's definitely coming. Can I do it now? Can I?'

Somehow that question at the end only makes everything sweeter. My orgasm pulses through my clenching pussy, again, again, too strong to take. I'm going to die of coming, I think.

Or maybe die of them saying stuff.

'Yeah, fill her. Do it. Oh, Bran, do it,' Tyler pants, but it's actually him who goes over. His cock jerks in my mouth and I feel the first hot spurt about a second before Brandon grunts his pleasure.

And then I'm just swamped by men, and the sounds of rough, prolonged orgasms, and the feel of cocks swelling and filling me to bursting. Tyler's hand goes to my hair and Brandon's to my hips, as they thrust and fuck and push me way past my limit.

My limit was back there somewhere, in the storage cupboard downstairs.

My limit was five years ago, when Brandon lifted my top.

Though I find, as I sprawl back against the bed – come-soaked and near exhausted – that I don't care in the slightest. Come on, limits, I think. Show me what you got.

Chapter Eight

'Have you ever fucked each other?'

It's a question that's been on my mind since all of this started. I don't think it's unreasonable to ask – though both of them see to think it is. Because despite the fucking they've just given me and all the lurid fantasies I confessed to, Bran goes red and looks away.

And, for a second, I think Tyler's going to do the same.

Then he answers, as calm as always, 'A couple of times.'

He's got a hand in my hair, stroking idly close to my temple. It's good – soothing. Especially for this topic, which doesn't seem to be soothing Brandon at all. I have to put a hand behind myself and catch a hold of him before he decides he's going to leap off the bed.

'Could we maybe not talk about this?' he says, while I think of all the reasons why we should. Being honest with each other, forming a trusting bond ...

Because I'm desperately curious about every tiny kinky facet of their lives ...

'Did you plough him good?'

Tyler laughs. 'Yeah.'

'Was his ass nice and tight?'

'I don't know. All that dildo fucking he used to do kind of wore him out.'

'Ty!' Brandon says, but he doesn't get off the bed. And, even better, he doesn't deny what Tyler's saying. When I look at him, he just looks right back, half mortified, half something else.

Relieved, it looks like, to finally confess. I don't think they've ever actually talked about it, outside of actually doing it.

'You really do that?' I ask, and he kind of shrugs one shoulder. 'You like something in your ass?'

'Maybe,' he says. Then he adds with some apprehension, 'Does that weird you out?'

'I told you earlier that I masturbate while thinking about you using my body for a come dumpster. What do you think?'

He covers his eyes with one hand, but this time it has nothing to do with possible gayness and/or dildo usage. It's just plain old garden-variety concern for his own mental wellbeing.

'I think I shouldn't get turned on when you say things like that.'

'Which part?' Tyler asks, as that hand of his slides down from my hair and makes its way to one still exposed breast. I've honestly no idea why I haven't put any clothes back on, I really don't.

Aside from the fact that I was just hoping he'd do stuff like this. I want them to do stuff like this, instead of whatever Brandon's currently doing. I have to shift onto my stomach and use both hands, just to prise his fingers off his face.

'The come dumpster part,' he says, as he fights me to the death. 'Not the masturbation part.'

'You like the masturbation part, huh?' I say, and am delighted to find that once the hand is off his face, it's not averse to holding on to mine. We're actually doing something normal, like hand holding.

While discussing receptacles that people might jizz into. 'Is that OK?'

'Stop asking if things are OK. We've done enough of that. We've had five years of that. I want … you know, proper talking.'

'Yeah,' Tyler says, as he levers one arm behind his head. He even gazes pensively up at the ceiling, before continuing. 'We should probably discuss how we're going to organise our lives around this monumental life-changing decision we've made to be together.'

I don't think Brandon or I can stop ourselves. We both crank our heads around in slow motion, to give Tyler the most stunned look he's ever been levelled with. I'm only surprised he doesn't melt on contact with it.

Though it's scary enough on its own when he just stares back at us. He just stares and stares until I break out in hives and Brandon takes a breath, like he's working up to saying something. He's going to pick up where Tyler has just left off and start talking about white picket fences and garden gnomes and God knows what else, and we're all only saved by Tyler's sudden laughter.

'I'm just fucking with you. Let's talk about sex some more.'

I hate him.

Except for all the places where I love him half to death.

'Where were we again? Oh yeah, so you were masturbating …' he says to me, once Brandon and I have started breathing again.

'I wasn't masturbating.'

'So *Bran* was masturbating …'

He cocks a finger at Brandon, like we're talking about some quaint little college story that he hasn't heard before. *So Bran was in the library, when Mrs Wellman walked by with her skirt tucked into her knickers …*

Only you know. Mrs Wellman never walked by with her skirt tucked into her knickers. Instead there's just a lot of hidden sex stuff that we have to now discuss.

'Yeah, I was masturbating. I'm always masturbating. Everything starts off with me, masturbating.'

Tyler's faux-innocent expression turns into something a little slyer. And maybe a touch bemused, too, when he realises the following: 'You know, you say that like it's funny. But actually, everything really *does*. One day I caught you jerking off to a picture of Maisie –'

'Oh gross, guys – you had a picture of me?' I cut in, but of course Tyler just barrels right by me.

'– and the rest is history.'

It's OK, however. Brandon has it covered. 'So this has got nothing to do with you being a giant pervert who doesn't politely leave the room when he catches his best friend doing himself?'

'I don't think many people would have walked away from you doing *that*,' Tyler says, and then this feeling just comes over me. It's like I can't resist asking. I can't resist *him*. It's exactly as Brandon said – it's not like he makes you, exactly.

You just want to, even so.

'What was he doing?'

'He hadn't yet moved on to the hard stuff. He was just fingering himself, like the little slut he is.'

The hand goes back over Brandon's face, again – though this time he at least peeps out from between a couple of fingers. And he doesn't sound that horrified, when he works up to saying words. 'Oh, this is just my worst nightmare. You know how I said that I wanted to, like, write Maisie a love letter, back in college? It contained almost none of this information.'

Tyler crumples his face up at me in an expression I recognise as mild distaste.

'Yeah, it was mostly just boring stuff, about your hair and your eyes. "Oh, Maisie, I totally did not beg my best friend to mount me, because that picture of you with your cleavage out drove me all nuts."'

I really have to come back to this point again, despite the other twenty points in that last speech I'm still reeling over. 'Seriously. You guys had a *picture* of me? Was I mysteriously naked in this picture?'

'You were wearing that little sleep vest of yours. I'm surprised he didn't go blind from jerking off to it too often.'

'I wish I was blind *now*,' Brandon says, but he does it far, far too loudly. I'm starting to think the lady doth protest too much, and if his already rejuvenated erection is anything to go by, I'm right.

'And you were just the kind of friend to help him out, huh?' I say to Tyler, before delivering the kicker, complete with over-emphasis. 'By *mounting* him.'

'He didn't mount me,' Brandon complains, but Tyler just laughs uproariously. Yeah, he knew what he was doing choosing a word like that one all right.

Mount. *Jesus.*

114

'How do you want me to tell this story, then?' he asks.

Although Brandon keeps that spread hand over his face, he answers. I'm proud of him, for answering – especially like this: 'Just tell her I got really horny and then you alleviated that by rubbing my prostate repeatedly with something you happened to have on your person.'

In fact, I think I *love* him, for answering like that – and Tyler certainly does. He laughs that big laugh again, and hauls Brandon in for the kind of half-hug he used to give him all the time.

Though, of course, it has a little extra meaning now. I don't think it was just sport fucking between them. I think they … well, I think they're awfully fond of each other, at the very least. And if that worries me a little, there's not much I can do about it. I just have to deal with it, up to the point where Tyler hauls me in for a hug, too.

Oh, we're going to have some weird Christmases in our future.

'Look at you two,' he says, like a proud father with his two favourite puppies. 'My little sex toys.'

Yeah. Some really, really weird Christmases.

'I thought you wanted to be all respectful of me, and stuff,' I say, but I do it while nudging his testicles with my left knee, so really, who's fooling who here?

'If you keep doing that, I totally will be. Little to the right.'

115

'You like that?'

'I like any part of you that's touching any part of me.'

'How about now?' I try, while digging my knee in just a little harder. You know, right between his carelessly spread legs.

But Tyler stops me in my tracks again. I guess there's no kink too big, or too small.

'So that's what you're into. Well, for the record, Bran likes hair pulling and I enjoy biting. *Biting*.'

'Really? Did you pull his hair while you fucked him?'

Both of them turn to look at me, in a way that makes me wish I hadn't asked. I'm pretty sure the hand-over-the-face, shame-based portion of the evening is over.

'You really asking? Or are we still just fooling around?' Tyler asks.

I can't help noting that he's got his hand in Bran's hair, the way he had his hand in mine a moment ago. And Brandon is getting very pink, again. Very foggy-eyed. I think he's actually rubbing his head back into that slight pressure, after a while of it.

'I'm really asking.'

'You want me to give a demonstration?'

I can't say yes. But then again, I can't say no, exactly. I just watch Brandon's face for my cue – is he OK with this, or not? Is he bothered, or not? Unfortunate, really, that it's almost impossible to tell. He doesn't say *red rum*, and that's about it.

116

'I don't know,' I say, because that's safe. That's easy. 'What do you want to do?'

Tyler seems to consider for a full ten seconds before replying. Which just makes me think he had the answer pre-loaded – probably since the year we all met at university.

'I want you to get him ready for me,' he says, so that I'm no doubt at all. He's *definitely* had that answer pre-loaded since university.

And I've been carrying around some shame or prudery since then, too, because for a long moment I'm paralysed. I'm terrified. I can't even think of what he means, until he spells the whole thing out, and even then I move on autopilot.

'Go to the end of the bed, Maisie,' he says. Followed by something worse, something that isn't for me. It's for someone else, and yet somehow it buzzes through my body just as strongly.

'Get on your hands and knees, Bran,' he says, and oh Lord, Bran *does*. He barely even stops to think about it. He just kind of moans and fumbles around on the bed, the way I did not so long ago.

Though this time it's me manhandling someone. I actually put out a hand and steady him when it seems like he might slide sideways off the bed. And the second he's in some kind of fairly obvious position – on all fours, like an animal, ready to rut – I do other things I didn't know I was capable of.

I run one rude hand over the smooth curve of his upturned ass, squeezing as I go – just a little bit. Just enough to make it a grope instead of anything more tame.

Tame wouldn't force that groan out of him, I'm sure. Tame wouldn't persuade him to spread his legs like a whore, before I've said anything else.

Though Tyler goes with it anyway. 'That's it,' he says. 'Spread those legs. Show her what you've got.'

It's quite possibly the most arousing thing I've ever heard, and I'm not sure why. Is it because it's a *man* Tyler's talking to, rather than a woman? It's definitely the kind of thing I'm used to hearing applied to some sluttish chick, as opposed to Brandon. Big, hairy, solid Brandon.

And yet I don't think it's that. I'm not even sure it's the sight of him that arouses me – that long, smooth, pale back, arched for me. The spread of his legs, the spread of his firm, tight ass cheeks, the swell of his swollen balls between.

No, no. I mean, these things *are* electrically exciting. But they're not half as exciting as the hand Tyler's got in his hair, or the way he turns his best friend's head, before plundering that neat little mouth with his own.

That's right. *They make out in front of me.*

And I have no idea how to respond to it. A big part of me sizzles with something like jealousy – thinking of those couple of fucks, of those moments they've had together while I stupidly exiled myself – but said jealousy wars with something far stranger. It sets up enemy lines and engages in skirmishes, until I'm just this big mess of resentment and utter, utter arousal.

They don't even hold back. It's not a polite kiss. I see their tongues squirming around each other's and after a while it's fairly obvious that Tyler is trying to fuck Brandon's face. He doesn't let him come up for air until Bran is gasping for breath and shaking a little, and more than that ...

He definitely wants me to do something to him.

Definitely. It's just kind of hard to tell what, because I'm not a guy. I'm pretty sure a guy would know exactly what to do, if he had a person on all fours in front of him and the person on all fours in front of him was rutting back against nothing, just begging to be filled.

But it's understandable that I'm less certain – I don't have anything to fill him *with*. I don't even have a dildo or a handy vegetable of some type. I've just got my own paltry little fingers, and a complete lack of lube, and this feeling in my chest like I'm about to burst.

I don't know, I don't know, I can't, I think, even if other people are sure I can.

'What are you waiting for?' Tyler asks, as though I'm knelt in front of something far less threatening, like a swing set. *Go on, Maisie. Get on the swing.* 'Lick him. Lick that tight little asshole of his.'

Disappointing, really, that I can't seem to go for it. I just kneel there, half shivering, unsure – head full of all the ways this could go wrong. What if I don't do it right? What if he doesn't like it?

What if he moans for me to do it, thirty seconds after Tyler's suggested it?

Because he does. He ruts back against me and fists his hands in the sheets, then practically *tells* me to do it. I've got two guys ordering me around, it seems, though I'm struggling to obey either. I close my eyes and fumble forwards, heart pounding.

Then I lick, quick and sharp, between the cheeks of his ass, and at the same time he makes a sound like someone drowning, and after that I'm lost.

I can't be anything else. I want him to make that sound again and, when he does, I do a whole bunch of things I didn't know I was capable of. I use my hands to spread his cheeks wider, for one – so that I can really get in there and rub the slick tip of my tongue over his clenched tight hole.

Which he seems to appreciate. 'Yeah, yeah,' he tells me. 'Just like that.'

But he doesn't mean *just like that* at all. He means *do more*, and I know he does because the moment I do he shudders for me. He groans and says my name and presses his face into Tyler's chest, and suddenly it's much easier to work on him. Easier, but a touch more embarrassing

– especially when Tyler asks what it is I'm doing.

I'm eating his pussy, I think at him, deliriously, but thankfully Brandon's there to supply some sanity.

'She's fucking me with her tongue,' he says, which I suppose is true. I'm certainly not hanging around any more. I'm tasting him – all earthy and salt-sweet, and not like I expected at all. I thought I'd get a lewd reminder of this nasty thing I'm doing, but instead it's just unbearably hot and Brandon's squirming and saying things like 'Uhhh you're making me so hard.'

Which only pushes me on. I spit wetly over that now glistening hole, and when Tyler says something unforgivably rude like 'Try him out for me' – as though Brandon really is his sex toy, moaning and shivering and ready to be used – I don't hesitate. I take the bottle of lube he passes me, and make a real mess with it between the spread cheeks of Brandon's ass.

Then I do the same to myself. I get it all down me and all over my hands, to the point where Tyler stops focusing on Brandon's ass and the mouth Brandon's pressing wetly to his chest, and starts focusing on me.

'Yeah,' he tells me, and I note that he's stroking his thick ruddy cock while he does so. 'Oil your tits for me. Get yourself all slippery.'

And I do. I work that slickness all over my stiff nipples and between my legs, and by the time I'm done I feel the way I look.

Wanton. Too turned on to bear it. My clit is standing stiff again, ready to be stroked, while my head fills with every variation we could try. Tyler could fuck Brandon and I could fuck him and he could fuck me and I could suck this as he sucks that and … oh, I don't even know what my pronouns are referring to any more.

There could be seven other men in here with me. It feels like there are seven other men when Tyler talks.

'Just ease in slow, slow,' he says, voice like a hum that burrows beneath my skin. He makes it so easy, just as Brandon said. All I have to do is lean into his words and urge my slippery finger against Brandon's asshole, and I'm there.

I'm fucking into his astonishingly smooth and far too tight passage without even really trying. And, Lord, you can tell he likes it. It's obvious right off, before I've squirmed another finger in and found something that makes him jerk and gasp and lurch towards Tyler's erection.

He likes all of it: the feel of something stretching him and twisting against that tight ring of muscle; the knowledge that it's me, exploring him; and, of course, the stiff cock Tyler then offers him.

'You want it?' Tyler asks, and I echo Brandon's response in my head. *Yes. Yes, I want your cock.* But I don't get anything other than a front-row seat, as Brandon licks and laps frantically around the taut, glossy head of Tyler's heavy cock.

God, he's going to split him in two. I know it, before he pushes him away and strides around the bed, that thick slab of meat still in his hand.

'That's enough, Maisie,' he says, but it's not the same sort of command he's been offering to date. This one's rough and guttural – impatient, I think. And I'm sure of it when he takes my place between Brandon's legs.

He's breathing too hard – obviously so. And he doesn't just stroke and then slowly sink in. He gets hold of Bran's thighs and yanks until Bran's face is in the duvet, and all the while Bran's making these noises. These desperate, horny sorts of noises, that only emphasise what's going to happen to him. He's got his ass in the air and Tyler's scissoring his fingers in that place I barely dared touch – it's really pretty clear, without anyone saying.

But Tyler does anyway. He always does. I think he likes a running commentary, as much as he likes the act itself.

'You ready to take my cock, slut?' he asks, then follows it with something even better: 'Tell Maisie how much you want it.'

I mean … seriously. Does Brandon have to do that? I think I'm going to pass out if Brandon goes ahead and does that while Tyler looks and looks at me with those sultry eyes. He has a hand on Brandon's back and, as I hold my breath and wait for the words, he strokes a hand down over the body in front of him, like he's posing it to its best advantage.

He wants me to enjoy it, I think. He wants me to feel included. And I'm proven right, a moment later. Brandon groans ecstatically that it's true, that he can't wait to be filled, and once Tyler is satisfied with his enthusiasm he says to me: 'Watch. Come here and watch.'

And I do. I almost collapse right into him I'm leaning over so hard, but that's OK. As he works that big cock of his into Brandon's resisting ass, he tilts sideways, and kisses the curve of my jaw, my cheek, my throat. He kisses every single place that won't impede his view of him spreading Bran open.

And I've got to appreciate that. He's a real gentleman when it comes to kinky sex stuff.

'You like that?' he says, and for the first time I actually know what to tell him right off. I don't feel as though I'm intruding, or like he's talking around me. The words just come out in a rush, over the top of Brandon's excited moans.

'I love it,' I murmur. 'I love seeing you take him.'

I think of that word over and over: 'take', as Tyler tells me more.

'He's so tight. I can hardly ease my way in.'

'Yeah, yeah. Go on,' I say, but I make a fatal mistake when I do. I completely forget all of those curve balls Tyler's so fond of.

'Are you this tight, baby?' he purrs and, as he lets the words slide out – so innocent sounding, so simple, really

124

– he runs a hand down over my ass to give it a playful little squeeze.

He pushes one slippery little finger down into the cleft between, rubbing and stroking, until I burn an even brighter red than I already am. My body glows and everything tingles there, viciously, when he presses firmly over one particular spot.

And then he spells it out. 'Ever had someone, there?' he asks, and I'm ashamed – though not for obvious reasons. I'm not really all that mortified over him touching me there, or that he's doing it as he slowly slides his dick back and forth in Brandon's tight ass. I'm not even particularly fussed that Bran has started moaning things like 'Oh yeah, use me, fill me up.' No – I'm really more concerned that Brandon, uptight dork extraordinaire, has had anal sex before I have. And I just can't admit that.

'Yes,' I say, but I don't know why I bother.

Brandon is currently getting reamed so thoroughly he can barely move from the position he's in, trapped between Tyler's big hands and the bed and that cock pumping roughly in and out. And yet he still manages to gasp out, 'She's lying.'

Apparently, I'm so obvious that a man whose cock is now making wet trails on the duvet can tell when I'm being dishonest. And another man – one who is shuddering over the feel of his swollen cock in another man's ass – knows it, too.

Tyler laughs, in spite of the squirming and rutting Brandon's now doing – so jerky and eager and delicious looking – and gives it to me straight: 'Did that ass fucking you supposedly took happen in your head, while you were masturbating?'

I get a flash of the last time I fantasised about something like that. Three men looming over me ... or was it four? Then all of them filling every hole I have, all at once. Most of them moaning about how they were going to pump me full of hot come, soon, that my ass was so sweet and tight and my mouth so hot and wet.

It's pretty embarrassing, and worse – I think Tyler can read it on my face.

'We could do what you asked for, you know,' he says, and then I'm sure he can read it on my face. I somehow secretly told him about my desire for a five-way, with some anonymous grunts. 'Only ... more like ... Brand gets fucked in the ass, first ... and then you second.'

Or maybe he just wants to offer something that makes Bran briefly panic.

'Are you serious? Ty, hold on a minute. Just hold on,' he tries, though his efforts are somewhat in vain. He turns his head so we can both see him, and there's absolutely no strength in his expression. He looks dazed, red-faced ... 'She's too small,' he says.

These words are followed by an obvious moan of excitement and I can't really tell if it is the feel of Tyler pounding into him that makes him cry out, or that one electric thought:

I'm too small. He's a monster; he'll split me in two. He'll get me like this on the bed – two hands on my upturned ass, pushing down hard until everything opens for him. And then he'll shove that cock of his in, again and again and again, like a fucking piston until I die of it. Oh God, let me die of it.

I think Brandon might be dying of it.

'Oh yeah, he's gonna come,' Tyler says, and though I want to ask him how he knows I'm inclined to agree. The sounds Bran's making are almost unearthly, and he's shoving most of them into the hunk of forearm he's biting down on. Plus, I'm pretty sure I can see how tightly he's clenching around that thick length, before Tyler expands on this point.

'Yeah, that's it,' he says. 'Squeeze me off, slut. Show Maisie how much you love it. You want to come in her mouth, huh?'

Oh God, yes please, oh please, let him come in my mouth, my mind babbles, but it needn't worry. Tyler's got it all under control.

'Here, come on – get up. Get back here,' he says. He shoves a hand into Brandon's hair and yanks him up onto his knees – so I can see everything clearly. I take in the gleaming slope of Brandon's torso, and the curve of his neck as he arches back into Tyler's body ... and, of course, his fit-to-bursting cock.

Lord, I don't think I've ever seen anyone as hard and stiff and red as his curving dick looks. It's almost kissing his belly, and the second I see it I *ache* to take it in my mouth. I actually ache. He needs some relief, I think – all that fucking, with nowhere to go. Only somehow, I've caught the wrong end of the stick again.

Tyler doesn't want me to suck Bran off until he comes. Oh no no no.

He wants me to *watch*, as Brandon goes completely rigid and makes a sound like someone straining up an immense hill, and then finally, oh finally … His cock jerks once, twice, as it spurts a thick streamer of come all over the duvet.

And it doesn't stop there either. Tyler even gets the chance to grin at me and tell me 'Told you so,' in the middle of the century-long orgasm Brandon's currently going through. I didn't realise a man could come like that, so hard and so extensively and with nothing touching his cock, but he can and he does and, once he's almost done, I lean down to let him finish in my mouth.

Or all over my mouth, if I'm honest. He misses most of the open part and coats my cheeks and my chin, too, so that I'm just one big nasty mess, again. I'm covered in lube and come – not to mention the slickness between my own legs, which now seems to be all over my thighs, too.

I want to touch myself so badly I almost do it.

And that's how Tyler finds me – sprawled on the bed with my hand on my arousal-slicked mound. After a while Brandon collapses next to me, and then we're just a couple of slutty bookends. Him dazed and probably lying in his own jizz, me still licking that same mess off my lips.

'You two dirty fuckers,' Tyler says, and, I'll be honest, I'm not even sure how to defend myself against that accusation. I *am* a dirty fucker. I'm so dirty that I don't stop rubbing at the slipperiness I've made, all over my plump, pouting pussy lips.

And I watch him too.

I watch him shamelessly, as he swaps the condom on his still unspent cock – though I can't be blamed. He's definitely putting on a show for me, again. He even bares his teeth as he stalks around the bed, like some predator just waiting for his prey to make the wrong move.

If I try to run he'll go for me. He'll get me by the haunches and do that word I can't stop thinking about – that one word I'd thought was funny, at the time, but now isn't.

Mount, I think. Mount me.

But he keeps me waiting.

'Kiss her clean,' he says to Brandon, and my cunt fizzes and pops at the thought of what he might mean. He could be talking about my molten pussy, which now feels as though it hasn't been touched since the dawn of time, despite the fact that it was touched about twenty minutes ago.

Or he could be talking about my mouth – and he is. Because a moment later, Brandon leans over – still trembling and blank-eyed from that soul-shaking orgasm – and kisses me tenderly there. He takes my chin between his fingers and flicks his tongue out to gather the last of himself off my skin.

Funny, but I want to keep it with me then. I kiss him harder, with all of my mouth and my hands, and I don't think about what Tyler is doing until Bran pulls away and says, 'You don't have to, if you don't want to.'

And then I have to think about it, because Tyler yanks me down the bed. He does more than that, in fact. He flips me over as though I'm made of nothing at all, while Brandon directs his protestations at someone else. 'She doesn't have to,' he says to Tyler. 'She doesn't have to.'

But he's wrong, and made even more so as Tyler says, 'I tell you what, if she doesn't want to, she can just say the same thing you do: red rum.'

I wonder why that word. Is it because of the movie? Or because it's the colour of passion and the sense of something intoxicating? Or is it because it's murder, backwards?

I'm murdering my old life, in which I did not allow a man to rub his slick thumb back and forth over my asshole, while another man eyes me with faithful nervousness. And I'm moving into this new life, in which Brandon whispers to me that he loves me, as he pushes a hand through my now ruinous hair.

I'm a tangled disaster, I think.

And I'm happy this way.

'Go on,' I tell Tyler, because he doesn't have to make me at all. He can just do it – pushing and stroking until my slick hole starts to give in under this strange new pressure – and he can say things, too, while he does it. I like his things, as much as I like that *I love you*. I more than like that *I love you*. I more than like this.

'Open up,' he says, and I like it even better then. I can feel the blunt head of his cock pressing and pressing against my entrance and, when I finally let him ease in – all too slick and too tense – it's a relief.

I sob, once, to the tune of Brandon saying, 'Careful, careful.'

'Is that what you want, Maisie?' Tyler pants, in some kind of reply. 'You want careful?'

But I can tell he already knows I don't. I'm bunching the sheets into fists, just as Brandon did. And the moment Brandon moves close to me, I claw at his mouth with mine – so greedy, suddenly. When did I get this greedy?

I don't know, but it feels incredible. The sensation of being stretched and used to capacity, of those hands on my hips pulling me back and back, in a telling, too-quick rhythm. He's going to come soon – I can tell that before he says a word. It's in his rough movements, almost too much for a while and then slicker, easier. And it's in the way he's moaning, just as Brandon did – with that same abandonment and eagerness.

I've never heard Tyler be like that before.

Unless he's actually putting it into sentences.

'Oh, she's so tight – you wouldn't believe,' he groans, as he finds a kind of jerking back and forth that seems to suit him best. He isn't going too deep into me, but I can feel what he is doing – he's rubbing the sensitive ridge around the head of his cock against my stretched hole, each stroke catching the rim in a very particular sort of way.

It hurts. Just a little. Just enough to make me moan back at him and beg him for more. Be harder, be ruder, use my ass, I think at him, but all he gives me are more filthy and maddening words.

'She's practically clinging to my cock. Yeah, Maisie. That good, huh? You like something in your ass?'

I do, I do.

'You want something else, huh? Maybe you want what we talked about. You want Bran to lick your sweet pussy while I fill this tight little hole?'

He's a goddamned mind-reader, I swear, because although this is amazing and arousing and I'm near beside myself, I know I can't come like this. I need Bran to do what he then does without comment, so frantic for it it's like he hasn't orgasmed at all. He's as fresh as a daisy and ready to lick my swollen cunt the second Tyler eases up and gives him space.

And he does it so well. He spreads my slit the same way Tyler's spreading my ass, firm and sure, then just laps a little at my stiff bead. He backs off when I nearly punch him then leans in again – and, oh, this time it's just right. It's just the right amount of pressure on the tip of my clit, back and forth, as Tyler says something insanely arousing like 'Ahhh, I'm gonna shoot in your ass.'

'You ready, Maisie?' he asks, which is hilarious, really. It's him who doesn't sound ready. He's panting and moaning, and the hands on my hips are slippery now. Whatever this is, it's going to hit him hard.

And, oh boy, does it ever. I'm caught momentarily between two sensations I can't bear to experience – the slide of Bran's tongue around my clit, and the feel of Tyler swelling and jerking in my ass. I'm not quite sure how to respond. I can't back away or move forwards. I can't escape.

I just have to endure the pleasure as it ebbs outwards from my pulsing clit, and ends up somewhere close to the shove and thrust of Tyler's cock.

'Uhhhh I'm coming, I'm coming,' he tells me, but he doesn't need to. The ring of muscle around him is sensitive, and I can make out every little stutter and jerk as his cock spurts and fills the condom.

And then it's over. It's over. It's done.

Only this time when we lie on the bed together, I have no urge to watch where my hands are going, no sense that I need to take eight showers immediately, to think things through.

I only know this:

I'm done eroding everything. From now on I'm rebuilding, instead.

Chapter Nine

Tyler's different now, and I know it. I know it the second he slips his hand inside my dress and fondles my bare breast, right there in his own crowded bar. People are looking, I think, though I don't know for sure.

I'm too busy moaning into his mouth, as he gropes me and swamps me and makes me his.

Because that's what this is, isn't it? A hallmark of ownership? I'm his little pet, now, his little toy, and that means I basically go limp the moment he does something beyond *making out in a public place*.

Though I get some of my senses back when I notice Brandon's not sat next to us any more. And I noticed he wasn't sitting next to us the night before, either, after a while of the kind of games Tyler likes to play. A three-some's a tricky thing to negotiate, it seems.

Who knew?

'I should go see where Brandon is,' I say, but Tyler just laughs. Which is the main problem really. We've kept our grips on this whole thing for a couple of weeks, but the grip is tenuous. One false move, one bit of laughing carelessness, and it could all go to hell – and I don't want it to. I'm seriously *this* close to quitting my job and taking Tyler's bullshit offer.

Be our publicist, he'd said. But what he really meant was *be our sex slave*.

And I'm surprisingly down with that. Last night, they made me come so many times I forgot my own name. Once they were through, I actually fell off the bed. I just slid right off, as though all of my bones had fled my body and left me with a sort of gelatinous mess.

But that's fine. It's good. I *want* to be a gelatinous mess.

What's *not* as good is Brandon's tendency to freak out a little bit. It's as though he's experiencing all the feelings I probably should, on top of his own.

'He's fine,' Tyler tells me. Unfortunately, the hand he keeps on my boob makes me doubt the veracity of what he's saying.

'Are you just going to keep telling yourself that until he has a meltdown?'

'Probably.'

'Tyler ...'

'He's just jealous,' he says, as though *jealous* is really a code word for *awesome*. Thankfully, I still know it isn't. 'That's not a *good* thing.'

'Why not? He likes being jealous.'

'Nobody *likes* being jealous.'

Tyler raises an eyebrow at me. It's his very best 'you can't be this naive' expression, and I brace myself for impact. 'They probably do if they're into cuckolding. But carry on. I think he enjoys your desperate efforts to make it up to him, too.'

I have to take a drink. A long one. Shame it's just lemonade. 'I'm so out of my depth,' I say, and though that's hard for me to admit in front of the Sexual Svengali over here, Tyler just smiles, faintly, to hear it.

'It would seem so. That's part of the fun though, isn't it?'

I eye him warily. If I say no, I'm going to have to go back to being a librarian. If I say yes, he could just fuck my ass again – only this time he might do it right in the middle of this bar. How far out of my depth does he want me to go, exactly?

'Yeah, but maybe it's not always fun for Brandon. I don't want him to feel ... forced into something.'

'Is that what you think is going on?'

'Well, sometimes he seems really uncomfortable.'

137

'And you think he doesn't want to be uncomfortable? He wants to be secure and safe?'

I'm not sure who we're talking about any more. 'No, not exactly. I just want to reassure him, sometimes. Tell him ... you know ... that I ... that I love him.'

It feels weird to admit it to Tyler before I admit it to Brandon, but somehow I can't help it. The words just spill out when I'm faced with Tyler's calm and steady version of persuasion.

And then I'm left with a lifetime to regret it.

'You love him?' he asks, and I can hear it, right there at the back. That slight change in his otherwise sturdy voice.

'Of course I do,' I say, but his expression doesn't change. It freezes in one default position – complete control, I'll call it – and remains there. I have to change the subject, slightly, just to make everything less nerve-shredding. 'Don't you?'

He shifts in his seat and, for the first time since this started, he looks away from me. Which probably means it's not any less nerve-shredding, at all. It's actually more nerve-shredding, because now he's going to open up or expose himself in some way, and I won't know what to do with this new, raw Tyler.

Or at least, that's what I think, until I hear his steely tone of voice. And his dismissive choice of words. 'Look, Maisie, what you've got to understand is ...'

That I can't love anyone. I'm an emotionally dead sex robot.

'... Brandon likes certain things. And I'm only too happy to give them to him.'

Now I'm on autopilot. A really, really bad sort of autopilot that makes me push for answers to things he doesn't really understand or want to know. 'But what if he wants more?'

'Then I'll give him that, too.'

He sounds so sure, so very sure. But I find I can't really believe him any more.

'Even if what he wants is for you to stop forcing him?'

He rolls his shoulders, irritated. Like I've got a finger under his skin, and I'm just burrowing and burrowing away until that facade finally cracks.

'Nobody gets *forced*. Is that what it feels like, to you? *Force*?'

I consider, briefly. I consider his voice like a silken rope, and his broad hands spread over my body. *You want to turn over, don't you, Maisie*, he says, in my head – and I know the answer.

'No. No. But I don't know how *Brandon* feels.'

He turns back to me – those eyes of his burning bright suddenly. The itch beneath his skin is gone, and this is what I'm left with: empty hands and no will to do anything, anything but what he says.

'I'll tell you how he feels: like he doesn't have to be

in control of his own desires. And because of that, it doesn't matter what those desires are. He's abandoned responsibility for them, and handed it over to me.' He leans in close, and traces one finger over the curl that's come loose, from the topknot I tried. 'Now doesn't that feel good? Doesn't that feel like a relief?'

'To what?' I ask, and am embarrassed to find my voice has gone all breathless.

'To let go. To let someone else carry the burden.'

He's right. It does. Most of my body has felt around twenty pounds lighter since last Sunday. 'Go on,' he'd said. 'You can if you want to. Who's going to stop you?'

No one, I think. No one but me.

'Yes.'

'And as you probably know by now, Brandon's burden is pretty big. He worries that he's gay; he worries that he's straight. He worries that he's warped inside, because it turns him on when I fuck you and tell him how much you enjoy my big fat cock.'

Brandon's not alone on that score.

I enjoy it, too – though one thing lingers in my mind, as I do. The tangled memories of the things we've done flicker through my head, and end on this one point. This one thing I hadn't considered, in the middle of all my concern about Brandon and how he's feeling.

'And what about you?' I ask, and when I do I meet his heavy-lidded gaze. I meet it dead on, in a way that almost makes him pull back. 'What do you worry about? What's your burden?'

His eyes drop before mine do, and I don't mind admitting I thrill in a way I hadn't fully considered, in amongst all of this submission.

'I don't know.'

I lean in close, as he did not a moment before. Just to, you know … try it out. 'You do know. Tell me. Tell me what kinky thing you'd like me to do, when your conscience isn't looking.'

'There's nothing,' he says, but he's lying. I can feel it buzzing through him, when I press a kiss to the curve of his throat and slide one hand inside the V of his shirt.

'If you tell me,' I whisper. 'I might do it.'

And then he gives it up, just like that. Just as I would if the positions were reversed. He's right – it's so easy when someone else takes the reins, takes control, lets you know that you don't have to do anything but say the words he gives to me, without hesitation: 'Make me.'

* * *

There's just one problem I hadn't fully considered when I squeezed those two words out of Tyler. It's very easy to be the one under control – of course it is! That's the whole point. You give up everything you are and just allow someone else to do all the thinking for you, for a brief time.

141

But being the one *in* control ... that's much, much harder. I suddenly find myself fumbling in the dark, completely unsure of what he might want me to do, but certain I want to do it, whatever it may be.

I want to give him it, if he craves it so. And he does, because the second we get up to the apartment he disappears into the kitchen, leaving me on the couch with Brandon – just like back in college, only with the pieces moved around. And Brandon, of course, gives me a look. He already knows before we've said a word or done a thing, I can tell. He can feel the shift in power, but that's OK.

I can feel it too.

It's what's terrifying me.

'Is everything OK?' Brandon asks, and I have to think, really think about what I should say, here. How does Tyler start things off, exactly? What did he say to Brandon, all those years ago, on a couch very like this one?

And then I remember. He *teased* him.

'You'll never guess what he did to me downstairs.'

Brandon gives me this wary look, but here's the thing – somehow, it only spurs me on. I look at those suddenly parted lips of his and his faintly wide eyes, and I want to carry on.

'What?'

'He fondled my breasts, while everyone watched.'

And OK, that's a slight exaggeration. But who gives a shit when Brandon's expression goes like that? It's not even an expression, really. It's as if his face falls down somewhere inside him.

'Are you serious?' he asks, but I can tell he knows I am.

'Yeah. And then he slid a hand under my dress, and stroked my clit until I came all over his hand.'

I think I'm getting the hang of this. It's all about playing as hard and fast as you can, until the other person breaks – like a really aggressive game of poker. I've got nothing but a pair of twos and Brandon's got a full house, but he doesn't know that. I can't let him know that.

'You're lying. Are you lying?'

'I don't know,' I say, as I trace the curl of hair that's made its way over his ear – just as Tyler did to me. 'Which would you prefer?'

'What's going on, Maisie? How come he's in the kitchen? He never goes in the kitchen. I don't even think he knows what a kitchen is.'

'We can talk about that, if you want,' I say, before glancing pointedly at his crotch. There's definitely something there after all, and I want him to know I know it. 'Or we can talk about whether you're hard, or not.'

'Maisie …'

'Are you?'

'Am I what?'

'Are you hard?'

He rolls his shoulders, like he's getting a kink out of his back. 'Yeah,' he says, because really, what else can he do? He can't lie. His cock is already pressing at the material of the sweatpants he's changed into.

'Are you thinking about him, or me?'

This time there's no shoulder roll. No glancing away, towards the kitchen.

'Both of you.'

'Are you sure? Maybe you'd like me to talk about what I did to him, rather than what he did to me.'

'Maybe,' he says, and I can hear the waiting at the end of his words. He's staring at some point just past my shoulder, now, but I know why. He's imagining it before I get to the good stuff, and when I do he slides a hand down over the ridge of his stiff cock.

'You want to hear that I sucked him off in front of everyone? They all just stood around and watched him fuck my face, and, when he creamed all over my bare tits, they applauded.'

'OK, I *know* you're making this stuff up, now,' he says, but the beautiful thing about it is that he doesn't sound sure. I don't think he *wants* to be sure.

'Does it matter?'

'Not really,' he says, and I can understand why. He's lifting his hips in time to the stroke of his own hand, now, and his cock looks like iron underneath his clothes.

144

He's getting close to that excited state in which he'll do just about anything, and more than that – so am I.

'So I can say something worse then? Something that would never happen in a million years, like *I bent him over one of the tables and bared that perfect ass of his, and then I forced a couple of the men down there in the bar to fuck that virgin hole.*'

'Jesus Christ, Maisie,' he says, but he doesn't put a hand over his face or stop with the light rubbing he's doing over the head of his cock.

Far from it. He sits up, instead, and puts a hand on one of my tits – which makes me wonder if that's what he did to Tyler, when Tyler got him riled up about me. Did he put a hand on Tyler's solid chest, and slide in close enough to mouth the heavy line of his jaw?

Maybe. Maybe.

'I bet he's so hot, and tight. You think he moans, to feel a thick cock in his ass? You think he'd moan if I fucked his ass? I could take him with a nice big dildo, while he fucks your hole, or your mouth. What do you think?'

He shudders all over, as he makes this wet, sloppy trail over my throat and down, down to my cleavage.

'I think I'm gonna come in my pants if you keep talking like this. Did Tyler tell you to do this?'

'Does it sound like he did?'

'I don't know. He's never said anything like this before. I don't even know if he likes getting fucked.'

He finds one stiff nipple and worries it, back and forth, back and forth, which drives me just about crazy. My sex is already slick and swollen, and those tingles he's prompting are making it worse. Another moment and I'll be squirming and arching into his hot mouth, and then he'll know.

He'll see that I'm not in control at all. I just want him to finger my slick cunt and lick my taut nipples, and, finally, I want him to relieve this ache. God, I'm *aching*.

'That's such a pity, don't you think? Five years – more than that – and you've got no clue if he likes the feel of something stretching him, filling him, pumping in and out, nice and slow.'

'I'm not as good as finding out as he is,' Brandon protests, but I have to say, he's doing very well on his own, here. He's already pushed the plunging neckline of my dress aside and now he's lapping and lapping at one exposed breast, tongue finding and flicking over my spiky nipple, unerringly.

It makes me want to sob and grind against him, but I resist.

'Well, why don't we try now?' I say, just as Tyler strolls back into the room. Hands in his pockets. Everything about him feigning nonchalance in a way that disturbs me, just a touch.

For the first time I can really see the cracks underneath.

'Tell him to take all his clothes off,' I try and, to my delight, Brandon goes for it. He stutters and fumbles and doesn't seem to know quite what he's doing, but he goes for it anyway.

'Could you ... uh ... strip?' he asks, the question mark in there out of place, but not unwelcome.

Tyler seems both amused and aroused by it, and that's a good place to be. 'You want me to take my clothes off?'

Brandon nods, a touch too eagerly – though he makes up for it in the fondling department. He's still got a hand full of my bare breast, and the other one has completely outlined the shape of his cock beneath the material. I can make out the thick ridge around the swollen head, and there's a damp spot where he's already leaking pre-come.

As Tyler is. Tyler's more than leaking pre-come in fact. He's so excited that he can't seem to bear to touch his cock, once he's got the clothes off. He just sort of stands there, with this big red thing jutting out in front of him, a look on his face like nothing I've seen before.

It's blank, the way Brandon's expression sometimes gets. Blank and slack and ready to be fucked.

'So what do you want to do now, Bran?' I ask, but unfortunately Brandon seems a little past making decisions. The second Tyler's cock is out there he fumbles his own free, and starts jerking it, roughly and too fast.

Another couple of minutes of this separated-by-a-living-room circle jerk and he's going to come all over himself.

And I can't have that. Not before I enjoy this party I've somehow managed to throw.

'Maybe you want someone to do that for you?' I ask, and this time he moans a *yes* for me. However, I'm not sure he really expects me to go with what I then do. I think he's expecting my hands or my mouth on his cock, while Tyler watches, mired in frustration.

But that's not what he gets.

'You did hear that, didn't you, Tyler? He wants someone to do something about that solid, slippery erection he's got.' I pause for dramatic effect. Hell, Tyler gets away with it, so why shouldn't I? 'So why don't you come on over here and suck him off?'

Both guys moan at that, but in different ways. Brandon's is a sound of surprise and desperation, but Tyler's is richer, deeper. It speaks of uncharted depths and a submission he didn't know he wanted, and it follows through in his actions.

He starts out by taking faltering steps towards us. Then progresses to a slow descent all the way down to the ground, as though his legs can't quite hold him up. He needs to crawl, just to keep himself steady and whole.

And if he also needs it because it's arousing, to slink towards someone on hands and knees ... well, maybe I won't say anything about that.

I'll just say, 'Go on. Go on, take that hard cock in your mouth.'

And then, best of all, I get to watch as he does it. Brandon eases that solid thing down, a little, until Tyler can reach – even though he doesn't need to bother. Tyler is tall enough and greedy enough to get right between those legs and, once he's close, he simply slides those soft, plump lips around the head of Brandon's cock.

And he doesn't stop there. He doesn't just suckle on the tip a little, or give it a tiny lick. He takes the whole thing – all the way down to the base – and when Brandon jerks and mutters the kind of concerned protest he usually reserves for me, Tyler does it again.

He does it until he gags, but that only seems to spur him on. Clearly, he wants to choke on some cock – he's happy to go at it to the point where he's gasping for breath and drooling all over Brandon's stiff length – and I know how to give him what he's after. I'm thrilled to, considering all the ways in which I'm unsure. This is like a sign, a clue as to how I should go about things, and I appreciate it enough to follow through.

'Fuck his mouth,' I tell Brandon, and I am gratified to see that look on his face – that harried, nervous sort of look, which says he's afraid of hurting someone. Apparently, it's not just women who can be the damsels in distress to him.

149

It's anyone who might be about to get fucked, three ways from Sunday.

'Go on,' I say, and Tyler *mmphs* in approval.

The little sound isn't needed, however. His eyes are closed and his fingers are digging into Brandon's thighs, and I swear if he sucks any harder on that cock he's going to take it clean off. I've never seen someone blow someone with such excited enthusiasm – not even Brandon, on that first morning we spent together – and it only gets worse when Brandon finally gives in.

He rocks his hips a little, to test it out, and Tyler groans so loudly around the thick shaft in his mouth that I actually see the vibrations travel up Brandon's body. He jerks as though struck, and squeezes what seems to be my hand, though I don't know when he started holding it.

Somewhere around the point where Tyler started jacking off, maybe?

'You see what he's doing, don't you?' I whisper in Brandon's ear, despite the fact that Brandon barely seems to know what day it is. If I asked him his own name, I doubt he'd know it. He's got his cock deep in Tyler's mouth and his hand is in Tyler's hair, now, and after a moment of this he actually holds his friend in place so he can get in deeper. Fuck harder.

It's an arresting sight, and one I'm loath to interrupt – only I have to. They're both going to come if I don't put the brakes on things.

'He's masturbating, Bran. He's jerking off, while he sucks your cock. Don't you want to do anything about that?'

Brandon turns his head, lazily, but doesn't seem inclined to do anything.

Until I point out something detrimental to the way this could possibly go.

'If you don't, he's going to spurt all over the floor, and then what use is he going to be? He can't fuck my tight little pussy, if he's already done it right here, right now,' I say, but I haven't quite got him yet. Not yet. It takes work to turn someone on to the point where they don't even know what they're giving a yes to. 'And you can't fuck his virgin ass while he does it, either.'

Ahhh, there it is. There's the thing. I see it on his face immediately – a kind of wondering disbelief, mixed with pleasure over whatever Tyler's currently doing. Rubbing his tongue on that sensitive spot just below the head of his cock, I think. Followed by a lewd little lick, right into the still leaking slit at the tip.

'You want me to ...' Brandon starts and, though his faltering voice and reddening face are very enticing, they're not the things I pay attention to. I watch Tyler, instead, who has progressed from licking to putting on a filthy show for us both. He curls his tongue around the glossy, exposed head of Bran's cock, as he eyes me in this certain sort of way.

Yeah, do it, that gaze says.

So I push, until Brandon obeys.

'I want you to get him on all fours, and lube up that sweet ass of his. And then when you're done, I'm going to spread myself out on the floor, and he's going to fuck me.' I give the cock Tyler has recently exposed a stroke, revelling in the sticky feel of pre-come and Tyler's saliva. 'And you're going to fuck him, until he explodes inside my tight cunt.'

'Oh God, Maisie,' Brandon moans. 'Maisie, I didn't know you could talk like this.'

But he doesn't resist. The second I return with the condoms and some lube, he sets about his task with all the diligence of someone so excited he can barely speak. He can't even get to grips with Tyler's big body, and for a long agonising moment I have to sit there and watch him slaloming around on that broad back. Hands all slippery, face all red, Tyler doing his best not to get impatient.

I'd laugh, if I wasn't too aroused to do it.

Instead, I get down there with him – after all, I'm an old hand at this now. I can actually slide a finger into Tyler's excruciatingly tight hole without blushing or wondering if I'm doing it right, and when Tyler gasps in what could be mild humiliation I add a second one.

And then I fuck into him, slow and steady, as Brandon gazes down at everything, open-mouthed. God only knows what he's thinking. It's alarming to me to see Tyler so submissive – on his knees with his thighs spread, two fingers working in his tight hole – but it's got to be a whole other realm to Brandon.

He's been doing the man's bidding for five times as long as I have. Plus, he has no idea that this isn't anything but Tyler's bidding, now. He didn't hear the conversation down in the bar. He doesn't know that Tyler *wanted* me to make him.

All he knows is that I'm currently fucking into his friend, while reaching up for a kiss.

And, oh, he gives me one. He goes after my mouth like it's a life belt and he's drowning. He can't cope with the sight of this and the sound of Tyler moaning, gruffly, and most of all he doesn't know what to do when I offer him a condom.

'Go on. Fuck him nice and hard. I want to feel you through him,' I say, but he still doesn't seem to know. I have to roll the rubber onto him, shivering over every little wince and jerk he gives me.

He's so primed it's almost unbearable.

Though not half as unbearable as the way he looks when I guide his cock to Tyler's entrance. He keeps his eyes closed, as if it will help matters, somehow. He's not really doing this, if he's not looking. And the *flush* that's on him … it's an unholy mixture of excitement and shame, and it's somehow made its way to his navel.

Plus, there are his words.

'I'm going to come the second I slide inside,' he says, almost like a complaint. Then less of one when he feels that tightly clenched hole giving just a little under the press of his solid cock.

'I won't fit,' he tells me, squirming and agitated in a way I probably shouldn't find arousing. And yet I do. My nipples are diamond hard and, every time I do something or see something new – like the head of that bulging dick slowly easing into Tyler's slick passage – my pussy clenches sympathetically, around nothing.

I need something in me. God, I do. And I need it now, before Brandon's even acclimatised to the feel of something so grasping and greedy around his prick.

'Christ,' he says. 'He's like a fist.'

Only you know. He doesn't mean it in the bad way. He's not complaining any more, and nor is Tyler. No … Tyler has stopped that weird silence, and has regained his ability to say the filthiest things, spurred on by the way Brandon strokes into him, once, like an experiment.

An experiment that definitely pays off.

'Oh God, do that again. Fuck my ass. Fuck it, Bran,' he blurts out, and then just for good measure he grabs a hold of my right thigh. Drags me towards him like someone too hungry to wait.

At which point, I remember the latter half of the fantasy

I promised Bran. You know, the part where we make a daisy chain, even though the very idea of a daisy chain is completely terrifying to me. The last time I used those words in earnest, I was a kid in a field full of flowers.

Now I'm some sort of porn star, about to get fucked while someone else fucks the person who's fucking me.

Lord, there are a lot of F-words in that one sentence.

'Come here, Maisie,' Tyler says, because apparently he can't stay out of control for long. He has to reach out and get a hold of it again, even as someone else pounds into his ass hard enough to make him shake and gasp and occasionally say something really rude, like: 'Ohhh, he feels so solid, inside me. So thick. Is this what it felt like for you? Did you feel like this?'

'Like what?'

'Like a whore, being used for someone else's gratification.'

I'm honestly not sure what excites me more, here. That he's referring to me, or that he's feeling that exact same way right now. He's just a big body getting drilled, over and over, until he's mindless enough to grope at me – mouth on my tits and between my legs, briefly, while I hold on to enough sanity to get a condom on him.

'I'm gonna last about thirty seconds,' he moans, but that much is obvious. He's so shaky he can't even manage to manoeuvre between my legs – I have to do that for him, too. I ease beneath the cage of his poled arms, spread my legs around him, and, once I'm trapped beneath them both, I get a hold of his solid cock.

Much to his discomfort.

'No, not like that. Don't. Oh my God, don't. Oh my God, I can't believe this feels so good. Seriously, Maisie, just ...' he stutters, and then he simply levers his body down a little, until his heavy cock is pushing blindly through my slit.

I swear, the second that fat head strokes over my clit I almost scream. I have to clamp a hand over my mouth to keep it in. I know I'm not going to be able to take him forcing his way into my body. I've gone all rigid and tight, and Brandon's pushing down and down on his ass in a way that makes Tyler very heavy on me.

I really am trapped, I realise, and have no clue why this excites me even more. I've got two big men on me, and both of them are about ready to go off. I should be nervous, or at the very least tentative, but I'm not.

'Just fuck me, fuck me,' I babble and, after a moment I feel him, working his way in. Slow, at first, as I adjust around that swollen head. Then with more urgency.

'Ohhhhh,' he moans. 'Are you really this excited?'

And of course I know what he means. I can feel how plump and flushed my sex is, how slick I am, and how easy it is for him, once he's gotten past the first hurdle. He practically glides all the way in, so smooth and easy I could cry.

While Brandon holds himself above us both, waiting. Waiting.

I think it's killing him to wait.

So I put him out of his misery.

'Make me feel it,' I tell him and, oh, he does. He fucks in once, hard, and Tyler in turn fucks into me, then all three of us moan, like some sort of chain reaction. Brandon's cock shoves against what must be Tyler's prostate, if Tyler's response is anything to go by, and Tyler shoves into me.

I cry out and beg them both to go harder, before I die of wanting it. Oh, I want it. I want them both, right now, like this – hips churning and cocks as hard as iron, squirming and working sweatily over me until I really am dying.

Or coming.

Whichever comes first.

'Mmmm, yeah you're making me do it,' I think I say, though I can't be sure. I'm a mess of sensation, clinging to Tyler's shoulders, feeling each juddering thrust, and then finally, finally: the pleasure lets go. It bursts around Tyler's still working cock, prompting him into a kind of release I've never seen him give.

He doesn't even make a sound when it washes over him. He just squeezes his eyes tight shut and opens his mouth, wordlessly expressing what I've just experienced first hand—the most incredible orgasm of my life. It's so intense that I'm still feeling it a minute later, when Brandon grunts and tells us both what he's about to do.

'I'm going to go off,' he says, like it's some kind of miracle. At last, at last, he gets to come – and in Tyler's ass, no less.

But that's not the thing that I remember, once it's over and we're sprawled in a heap on the floor. Instead, I end up thinking of the look on Tyler's face when I say to him what I found pretty easy to say to Brandon. I give it to Bran after he's curled against my side, and told me those words again.

'I love you,' I say. 'I love you.'

Then I say it to Tyler, too.

And after his eyes have gone all startled and his body has finished tensing, I realise something pretty fundamental. It wasn't a joke, that thought I had. He really *is* an emotionless robot, enjoying the company of his two little sex pets.

And I'm a fool to imagine there's anything more.

I'm sure I'm a fool.

I'm a fool, aren't I?

Chapter Ten

I try to sneak out before both of them wake up. Mainly because I suspect – no, in fact I *know* – that if I say I need to go back home to get some stuff, they'll try to stop me. They'll suggest a road trip together, and then we'll pile into the car and probably end up having sex in my apartment, too, and I won't have a second to breathe.

I just need one second. A little slip of time, to get myself together and be certain that this is what I want, before returning.

Even though I know I don't really need any time at all. I spent last night writing, for the first time in years. I didn't think about the library, or my future – I didn't even really think about Tyler and Brandon. I just thought

159

about all the things my life could be now, if I wanted it enough.

I could have love, and sex, and happiness. I could actually work at this bar with my two best friends, and in the evenings … well. It's pretty obvious what's going to be happening in the evenings. And in the afternoons. And all the time.

Yeah, it's obvious all right.

I'm going to be the sort of person I always wished I was. Soon, soon – once I've gathered my shit together and called the library and done a bunch of other things. Tyler's said I can sublet, if I want, and live in this flat. But if I'm going to do that there's got to be arrangements made.

And furniture brought over. They don't even have a wardrobe, in here – though I think it says something that I hadn't noticed until now. I hadn't noticed a lot of things – like how closed off Tyler is, for example. I always thought he was really emphatic and open, an extrovert to Brandon's introvert.

But I guess things just seem that way, on the surface.

He definitely looks all surface, when he emerges from the bedroom and catches me in the act. A fake smile plasters itself over his face and he does something Tyler-esque, like clasping the back of a chair in his two big hands.

Look how immense I am, that move says. *Look how slick.*

Even if he doesn't seem that slick in his words. 'You going?' he asks, and I can hear the other question, underneath. *For good?*

Though for some reason, I don't feel like jumping to his rescue. Clearly, he's an emotional robot. He's not sure how to have feelings. But equally transparent is the idea that he wants me to stay.

In fact, I can make it out so keenly that my insides jump for joy. Tyler, handsome and golden and perfect, wants me – Maisie the Librarian – to stay.

'Well, I thought I might ...' I tell him, and then I do something very bad indeed. I don't finish the sentence, and instead leave him to fill in the rest: *Yeah, I could be going for good. What do you want to do about it? What do you want to say?*

Though I'm betting he'll go with something warm but slightly aloof, like *You know I'm very fond of you, Maisie* – and that's OK. It's enough to let me know that I'm not just here for sex toy reasons, and even if he can't quite go with it I can see it in his expression.

There's something like feeling there.

'So you're not going to take me up on the job offer?'

'Maybe.'

'And there's nothing I could do to persuade you either way?' he asks, though it's not the words that affect me. It's the way he glides towards me, slow and almost predatory. I'm pinned to the door before I know where

I am, but I have to say I don't mind in the slightest.

I don't mind any of this, and never have. He has to know I never have. I'll never leave him, or Bran, again – not ever.

'Make me,' I tell him, and he does. He looks at me with the same soft eyes Brandon always offers, and says the words I didn't think he could: 'I love you. I love you – stay.'

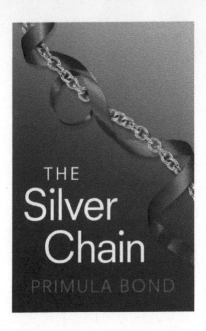

THE SILVER CHAIN – PRIMULA BOND

Good things come to those who wait…

After a chance meeting one evening, mysterious entrepreneur Gustav Levi and photographer Serena Folkes agree to a very special contract.

Gustav will launch Serena's photographic career at his gallery, but only if Serena agrees to become his companion.

To mark their agreement, Gustav gives Serena a bracelet and silver chain which binds them physically and symbolically. A sign that Serena is under Gustav's power.

As their passionate relationship intensifies, the silver chain pulls them closer together. But will Gustav's past tear them apart?

A passionate, unforgettable erotic romance for fans of *50 Shades of Grey* and Sylvia Day's *Crossfire Trilogy*.

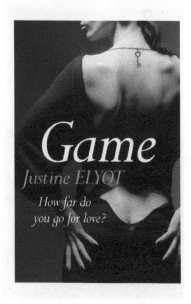

GAME – JUSTINE ELYOT

The stakes are high, the game is on.

In this sequel to Justine Elyot's bestselling *On Demand*, Sophie discovers a whole new world of daring sexual exploits.

Sophie's sexual tastes have always been a bit on the wild side – something her boyfriend Lloyd has always loved about her.

But Sophie gives Lloyd every part of her body except her heart. To win all of her, Lloyd challenges Sophie to live out her secret fantasies.

As the game intensifies, she experiments with all kinds of kinks and fetishes in a bid to understand what she really wants. But Lloyd feature in her final decision? Or will the ultimate risk he takes drive her away from him?

Find out more at www.mischiefbooks.com

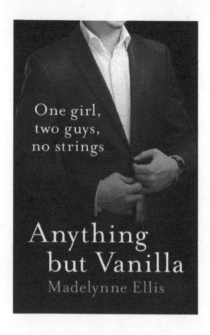

ANYTHING BUT VANILLA
MADELYNNE ELLIS

One girl, two guys, no strings.

Kara North is on the run. Fleeing from her controlling fiancé and a wedding she never wanted, she accepts the chance offer of refuge on Liddell Island, where she soon catches the eye of the island's owner, erotic photographer Ric Liddell.

But pleasure comes in more than one flavour when Zachary Blackwater, the charming ice-cream vendor also takes an interest, and wants more than just a tumble in the surf.

When Kara learns that the two men have been unlikely lovers for years, she becomes obsessed with the idea of a threesome.

Soon Kara is wondering how she ever considered committing herself to just one man.

Find out more at www.mischiefbooks.com